A tale o
the b
the roughness, pain, and hell of war;
and the goodness of humanity.

"A beautiful, elegant, poignant, and romantic WWII novel. The author's attention to detail and his poetic literary flair set him apart from others in the genre."

--David Aretha, award-winning author and editor

Song of Cigale

Cover art by Fantasia Frog Designs
Digital ISBN: 978-0-9971439-3-5
Paperback ISBN: 978-0-9971439-4-2
Hardback ISBN: 978-0-9971439-5-9

Song of Cigale

By

Mark Perretta

AUTHOR'S NOTE

This book is dedicated to my dear friend, classmate, and granddaughter of Staff-Sergeant Charles D. Warfield. SSG Warfield enlisted in the US Army on June 19, 1939. Beth would be born on the same day years later. SSG Warfield was assigned to Company "D," 1st Medical Battalion, and would serve in the following battles and campaigns: Tunisia, Sicily, Normandy, Northern France, Rhineland, Ardennes, and Central Europe.

SSG Warfield and the 1st Medical Battalion landed in the early afternoon on Omaha Beach on June 6, 1944, D-Day. Under heavy artillery and machine-gun fire from German fortifications, his unit remained on the beach treating the wounded for about an hour. Eventually, the unit made its way to the relative shelter at the base of the cliffs where they set up the Battalion Aid Station. They remained there overnight treating the wounded before moving inland.

SSG Warfield would be awarded the Good Conduct Medal, American Defense Service Medal, and the European-African Middle Eastern Service Medal for his efforts. His date of departure from Europe to the US was June 2, 1945. SSG Warfield would take a job at Abbott Laboratories until his retirement. He died in 1987.

While most people know of the events of June 6, 1944, many do not realize on August 15, there was a second D-Day in Southern France.

That is where *Song of Cigale* begins.

ONE
They Know!

France —July 1944

"*Cours!*" her mother cried. "Run, Caro! Run!"

Caroline's feet pounded the gravel path as she propelled herself into darkness. She was a whirlwind of limb and emotion, her short raven hair bouncing with each hasty stride. One unquestionable thought tore through her mind.

I must get to the loft!

The nineteen-year-old strained toward the beach, the distant boathouse feeling out of reach even as she pushed harder. On this night, the distance seemed interminable. Only when she skidded on soft sand and waves lapped beside her did she allow herself a conscious breath of relief. Ducking around the structure's corner, she aimed for the doorway. Tears blurred her vision, but she blinked them away and surged forward.

She slammed the door wide and threw herself onto the wooden ladder. Clutching the uppermost rung within reach, she clambered upward. In the black interior of the boathouse, her blue dress flapped against her rising form. Out of breath, she lunged into the loft and scrambled to the farthest corner before collapsing onto her back. Despite Caro's best efforts for silence, her chest heaved convulsively and the frantic beat of her heart, she worried, would be her undoing.

The Nazis have found us! They know!

Lying on a bed of straw, she reached overhead, her fingers trembling. She drew a quick breath and slid a single tile of terracotta roof away from its position, lowered it into the loft, and leaned it to the side. The aperture allowed a sliver of fresh air to find her cheek, and she welcomed it. Despite the distance from boathouse to home, sound trickled to her ears, allowing her to discern her parents' voices or anything warning her of danger.

Caro glanced through the hole directly above her. Skies were usually clear in La Ciotat, but tonight, the moonlight was especially crisp and brilliant. Stars crammed the heavens.

How? How did the Nazis find out?

Her breathing slowed but only for an instant.

Cars screeched. Doors slammed. And the echo of a pounding fist on the faraway house's wooden entrance shook her, even from her hiding place.

A silver locket hung from Caro's neck and clung to her heaving chest. Her hand flashed to the locket, and she twisted it between her index finger and thumb, a nervous habit begun shortly after Arthur had—

More pounding.

Only moments earlier she'd been in the cozy kitchen, washing dishes with her mother. Talking. Relaxing. The phone rang; her father answered. All color drained from his face.

And with one look, Maman knew. *I knew!*

Her maman had screamed, *Run, Caro!*

And she ran, just as they'd practiced.

But how? How did the Germans find out?

Her parents had told her repeatedly of the Maquis' price. This day may come, and when it did, to run and hide and wait...

And then?

To distract her troubled mind, she peered through the aperture and into the sky. Caro gulped the cool night air as she attempted to slow her breathing and steady a throbbing chest. *The moonlight is...wonderful.*

Words to a familiar children's song slipped from her dry lips. "*Au clair de la lune, Mon ami Pierrot...*" She caught herself. Though her lips continued to move, all must be silent. Caro strained to hear through the small opening above her.

My candle is dead. I have no more fire.

The routine was set; her parents had prepared well. Over the last year, many people's homes in town had been searched. Any resistance contraband, lack of German allegiance, or hint of impropriety was more than enough cause for arrest...or worse. In addition, Caro had also heard the stories of what could happen to young French women. They were easily targeted by German soldiers for only the unthinkable. Now, at nineteen, she had reached the age where *Papa et Maman* told her she must hide, like her brother before.

They will leave, like before. They must.

Fingering the locket Arthur had given her in that very spot, she unhooked the silver clasp. A moonbeam found its way through the hole in the roof and illuminated the photo taken on her birthday at L'Office'in, a favorite restaurant in the village. They'd eaten outside on the terrace overlooking the bay, and the memory, fresh as a Monet painting, seemed like only the day before. In reality, it had been over seven years earlier.

Before the Germans invaded.

Before this terrible war.

Her mother had made her an apple birthday cake with fluffy caramel icing. Her father had brought a present wrapped in blue paper and topped with a blue bow, her favorite color. And when she tore the paper off and discovered a postcard album of all the places in the world she would like to visit someday, she wished time itself would stop. At that moment, she prayed to God to always be this young and loved.

With her thoughts and emotions scrambling, she cupped the picture of her family tucked within the tiny metal frame, staring at the familiar faces. Then the terrible irony hit her. She held everything dearest in the world in the palms of her hands. And she could not lift a single finger to help any of them.

I wonder how Arthur is... I have not heard from my dear brother for so very long. He has to be—

Pop! Pop! Pop! Pop!

Four unmistakable cracks shattered the night air. The sudden, rhythmic cadence was not random like a sequence of firecrackers, and her eyes, once heavy with sleep, widened in horrified fear. A sickening certainty rushed through her. All hope collapsed into the pit of her stomach. She knew.

Everyone dearest to her heart was gone.

Only echoes of her parents' instructions and final words remained. No matter what you hear, what you think you hear, remember the plan. Stay where you are.

TWO
Lucky Lady

Somewhere over France —August 1944

The gaping bomb bay door glared back at him with an evil grin.

Moments before, the mission had been as normal as any other nighttime jump Michael had made. But the bullets of 20mm flak guns from a German night fighter ambushed their plane, shredding one of *Lucky Lady*'s wings. Then, one final time, the fighter blasted the coup de grâce. Gas tanks exploded, the B-24's bomb bay door ripped open, and the remaining wing, upper gun turret, and rear fuselage blazed in flames as the plane screamed toward earth.

In a cruel twist of irony, that same hole, the bomb bay, happened to be Michael's only way out. Like some bucking bronco, the plane rolled and heaved, casting him and Jim near the 11,000-foot abyss of darkness yet never close or steady enough to jump clear. *Lucky Lady* shuddered, her nose turned sharply, and the men slid like rag dolls.

But the fuselage bounced again, and, in an instant, they were tossed aft.

Flames from the rear main frame licked at Michael's boots. Shards of metal whizzed past his head. He glanced at Jim. His best friend's eyes shot wide with terror; his body sprawled only an armlength away. Smoke rolled through the bulkhead, and both soldiers shook with spasms of coughing. With instant certainty, Michael knew only seconds remained before the plane plunged below the dead zone, the height at which a parachute could safely deploy no longer. In a last-ditch effort to save both their lives, he lurched awkwardly, threw both arms out, and snatched Jim's parachute harness.

"Got it!" Clinging to the straps, he held firm. *Must pull Jim through bomb bay doors.* It would be their only chance to deploy their chutes and possibly survive.

Wind whipped and ear-splitting noise cracked throughout every crevice of the aircraft. The propellers roared, making any communication difficult, if not impossible.

Only inches from his friend's face, he screamed, "Jim! Come on! We've got to jump!"

He scanned the crowded, smoky interior. The radio operator struggled to free himself from a tangle of wires and equipment. The flight engineer slumped in a bloody heap. In the cockpit, two pilots battled the doomed plane, trying to steady her, the only thing they could do to buy a few precious seconds for what was left of the crew. Everyone else...*gone.*

Miraculously, the plane leveled for an instant, and at that moment, Michael threw his weight toward the lip of the bomb bay catwalk; his boots slid onto the precarious edge. He lowered his backside to the opening, knowing nothing but air and darkness loomed below. Michael squatted, preparing to push off the steel struts and thrust their bodies through the gaping hole.

He held an iron grip on his best friend's parachute harness. *Come on, Jim! I need to pull you out!*

But Jim's hands clung to a metal strut near the bay, and he refused to let go. His hollow gaze broke Michael's concentration. "Let go!" Michael screamed. "*Jim, let go!*"

Seconds crawled before Private First Class Jim Steele shook his head and mouthed, "I'm sorry."

Just as Michael kicked backward, trying to force their bodies through the aperture, Jim unclipped his parachute harness buckle, and it slipped lifelessly between Michael's fingers. When the last of the strap cleared his fingertips, he stared into Jim's gray eyes and recognized the look of a soldier giving up before the battle was lost. And as he plunged backward, into the void, in that final agonizing moment, he watched his best friend just stand there, accepting death. Raising his hand almost in salute, Jim vanished inside the plane.

The image would be seared in Michael's mind for eternity.

Michael tumbled clear of the B-24, grasped for his ripcord, and yanked. Slithering free, the chute took the wind and popped to life, and, with a sudden jerk, he floated. His descent slowing, he glimpsed the doomed plane. Tremendous forces of gravity plummeted *Lucky Lady*, splintering her burning body into pieces. Flames burst skyward as she exploded upon impact, scorching the night sky.

He'd believed his commanders. The invasion into Southern France, *Operation Dragoon*, had been planned to catch the Germans off guard. The twenty-four-year-old shook his head in disbelief. His commanders had been terribly wrong.

My God...my crew is gone.

Tilting his head to the heavens, he prayed. *Please, God, have mercy on their souls.* He noticed his leather gloves clenching the harness above. They were scorched with a dark-red stain. Blood. *Is it mine or Jim's?*

Doubt of survival flooded his mind, but so did vivid images of his parents.

C'mon, Michael...think.

Only darkness and uncertainty lay beneath his boot soles. Fear of the unknown gripped him. Would the wind carry him into the trees? Trees were better than touching down in an open field or too near a town, but the impact might fracture his back or break his neck.

Would the Germans find him dangling and shoot him as if exterminating some pesky crow? If they took him prisoner, he could still be executed on sight. Either way, options were quite limited wherever he landed.

With toes pointed and knees bent, he prepared for the shock of a sudden meeting with terra firma. A last gust of wind pushed him closer to a group of trees, though he could not tell their size or type. Michael worked the steering lines, but they provided little maneuverability.

Maybe I can swing my chute...there!

Cloth ripped, and a sharp tug snapped everything to an abrupt stop. Snagging a tree limb, the parachute held firm. Suspended in midair and bouncing, he stared beneath his boots. Michael felt like an unsuspecting fish after the hook had been set. The drop had to be at least twelve feet. Even in low light he could tell, still a very long way down. He considered his options. His time frame was clear.

The *Lucky Lady* would burn for hours, sending a column of smoke into the sky like a beacon for the enemy. And with the plane crash noticed, it was only a matter of time before someone, Gestapo or the Vichy police who collaborated with the Nazis in that area of France, arrived. He had to cut the harness and take his chances.

Yanking an army issue knife from its sheath in his right boot, he reached above his head and placed the serrated blade to the first harness.

What if I break an ankle or leg in the fall? The knife sawed through the first strap with ease. What if I'm never found...to die in oblivion?

His body bounced downward a few inches then steadied; the remaining straps held firm.

Deep breaths. Deep breaths!

Attention shifted to another leather harness, and he hacked at the thick strap and limp cords. Between his weight and lack of support from the harnesses, his body slid farther downward. He pondered how hard the fall would be.

I'm out of time.

Desperate, he sliced through the last shred of strap and plunged like a rock, slamming into the cold earth. A searing pain jolted through his legs and lower back. Spots of dazzling light danced before his eyes, same as when a shell exploded so near, its destruction could be tasted. He lay on the ground and tried to breathe but could not. Afraid to move for fear of something being shattered, he gasped, trying to settle his quivering nerves.

Get up! He rolled over and shuddered with pain. *Get up!*

Wiping a tender lip with his bloody glove, he rose to his knees, leaned on the tree that had snagged him, and searched for a knothole, something to grasp. Fingernails dug into leather gloves, leather gloves into tree bark, and he rose, but his legs almost buckled as new waves of pain tore through him. He bit his lip to stifle a scream, and a metallic taste filled his mouth.

Michael grasped his dire situation with the ringing clarity pain affords. A tired or injured soldier needed to fall back on his training and use his battle sense to persevere. That training had taught him there was only one objective. Avoid capture. Enemy soldiers would be fanning out their search patterns, looking for survivors from the crash. A branch extended half a foot from the base and provided the first step.

With wave after wave of agony crashing over him, he climbed, dropped the chute, and slid down the trunk. Five feet from the ground, the branch he clung to split, and he nose-dived into the parachute below.

Blood trickled from his nostrils, and the taste returned.

A warm, buzzing sensation, almost comforting, eased his light-headed mind. Numbness...everywhere.

Soft, like my pillow. I could just close my eyes and sleep. Just let it all be over.

An image of Mother and Father flashed. Dad had been his high school football coach, and, for a moment, Michael was back at practice. As the team's starting quarterback, he was used to getting hit and being facedown in the dirt.

Get up, Son! Dad blew his whistle.

Was it Father's whistle? His voice?

Michael woke with a sudden, violent jolt, his body shaking. He rolled onto his knees and balled up the parachute. Then, inch by agonizing inch, he pushed against the tree and forced himself to his feet. But his hamstrings locked, and a searing pain shot down the backs of his legs and into his toes. He sucked in a quick breath and ignored the agony.

A tree crevice provided ample room for the chute, and he stuffed it inside, hiding it from view.

Have to hurry.

Though darkness held the land, morning's first light illuminated the eastern sky. He staggered into a thicker grove of pine trees nearby. Even though Michael had traversed only a few hundred yards from his landing point, the agonizing pain drove him to his knees. Reaching for his belt buckle, he undid the clasp then pulled it two notches tighter in an effort to provide more support for his screaming leg muscles. It did not work. Instead, spikes of pain drove him down, onto the flat of his back. Tears welled as pain forced him to remain motionless. In misery, he bit his lower lip, stifling any shriek into a quiet whimper.

Lying on his back and unable to move, he searched the night sky. Tree boughs danced in the breeze, but, above him, a momentary clearing, and he peered directly to the heavens. Finding several constellations of stars, he focused on their beauty and position in the darkness. Then he pictured the final images of his best friend holding onto the metal strut of *Lucky Lady*, refusing to let go then disappearing forever. Maybe Jim was the lucky one.

Please, God, please help me. Just get me through this. Sarah...

He searched the distant dots of light and grimaced. Pain rolled from his legs and gripped his entire body.

Please, let me see my family, again. Sarah, my love...

He extended his right arm to the sky and raised an index finger. Pointing at one of seven stars, he traced a familiar pattern. From one white dot to the next, he connected each. "It's called the Plough."

His arm fell with a *thud*, his head rolled to the right, and all was still.

Thompsonville, Kansas—1938

"It's called the Plough!"

"The Plough? Like the one my grandpa uses on his farm?" Michael stretched out next to Sarah's slender body in the bed of Grandpa Luke's Ford pickup.

Sarah giggled. "No, silly. I learned about it in school. That's what they call it in England. It's a group of seven stars. And if you connect the dots, or stars, they form the Big Dipper and lead you to Polaris."

"Polaris?"

"You know, the North Star."

Michael caught scent of his girlfriend's perfume and breathed deeply, finding it hard to concentrate on anything else. "Oh! I see it." Giving up on the constellation lesson, he tilted his head and studied her profile instead. Even in the darkness, her eyes and shoulder-length hair sparkled in the moonlight. Tucked between her long, straight locks flowed a single stream of braided hair.

Love whispered wonderful things into Michael's ear. He listened completely and reflected on the evening.

Earlier, he had quarterbacked Thompsonville High to a 17-0 win. The victory propelled his team to a 4-1 record, which should keep Father in a good mood until Monday's practice. After the game, the couple enjoyed their ritual—into town for a cheeseburger and milkshake at Taggart's ice cream shop then a stop at Perry Lake for some late-night stargazing and perhaps a few stolen kisses before heading home.

"Some call it the Saucepan. They're *amazing*, aren't they?" Sarah glanced at him then back to the night sky.

The wonder on her face made his heart skip. He turned his head, and the vastness of heaven unfolded before his eyes. She was right. "I just can't believe how many there are!"

"It's a miracle, isn't it? And to think so many people ignore them, never remembering to just look up and see their beauty!"

But none as beautiful as you. An endless sea of stars stretched in the immense Kansas sky as the high school seniors lay flat on their backs.

Michael chuckled to himself at the sudden memory of how they met as freshmen, and how their courtship started soon after their first awkward conversation and shy dance at Fall Homecoming.

"What?" Sarah asked.

"Nothing. But it kind of makes you feel small, doesn't it?" He picked at a frayed thread of the woolen blanket beneath them. "Really small."

"It makes you wonder how God had time for me and you, when He created something like the stars."

Michael's head settled next to Sarah's, and his lips met the blush of her cheek. "How'd you get so smart?"

"*I* pay attention in class."

"So do I!" A chill rippled through Michael's shoulders. He leaned closer to his girlfriend. Warmth radiated from her flawless skin. He watched her chest rise and fall and couldn't remember ever being as content or intoxicated with love. It was pure joy.

Sarah laughed. "Now, here's the neat part. Give me your hand."

He slipped it into hers and she raised both their arms to the night sky. "If you trace the Big Dipper from the handle to the pan"—she slowly extended her index finger, and he did the same. Guiding his hand, she traced the constellation—the North Star will be five times higher than the pointers at the end of the pan."

"Neat."

"So, as long as you can find Polaris, you will never be lost. Especially to me." Their arms lowered to the bed of the truck; fingers intertwined.

Michael rolled onto his side and stared at his girlfriend's delicate features. "Sarah Johnson..."—he leaned in for a kiss—"I will love you forever."

THREE
Just Boys Still

Somewhere over France —August 1944

As the planes accelerated, racing into darkness, their furious growl descended, and the French coast shivered with sound. Sergeant Frank Taylor closed his eyes and imagined 396 C-47s streaking through the night.

This wave of impending doom required the immediate fantasy of at least a dozen hurricanes. Its deep and all-encompassing roar reverberated through Frank's being and shuddered the hull he leaned against. Soon, he would be one of 5000 parachutes plunging as one massive form.

Perhaps, God himself commanded a legion of apparitions from Heaven above to Earth below.

It was not the sort of arrival Frank had anticipated. The predawn jump lacked the benefit of moonlight, and a general haze hung thick in the air like a layer of white paint. Heavy ground fog disguised drop zones from danger zones. And the possibility of German fighter patrols added to a palpable sense of unsettling discomfort.

He squinted, peeking right then left. A French commando and twenty-six other American paratroopers sat crammed in every square inch of available space with body and equipment. Some men slept, some smoked, some prayed, and others checked their gear. A few talked quietly as they prepared to jump over Le Muy, France.

The twenty-three-year-old laid his chin on the reserve chute. Fastened across Frank's belly, the chute was pushed nearly to his jawline by the excessive equipment. He walked through a mental checklist. Flashes of rugged training, practice jumps, and previous missions intermingled with a certain eagerness that filtered through his body.

Then a single thought dominated his mind—*Let's get to the jump zone.*

His eyes grew heavy with fatigue despite the twinge of anxiety deep in his gut. The constant roar of engines and overpowering dimness inside a plane always seemed to have the same effect on Frank. Skirting the edge of sleep, he recalled the anger he'd felt after the bombing of Pearl Harbor and the pride that beamed from his parents' faces when he'd told them of his plans to enlist. And since then, despite a nagging fear he may never return home, he had proven himself as a soldier and leader, time and time again.

His eyelids closed, and his mind opened.

He was ten years old and climbing haystacks in the barn. His older brother Michael scampered ahead, just out of reach. It was a race to the top, and, despite Grandpa's warning not to "play on the stacks," climbing to this summit and declaring oneself king seemed a daily occurrence. Life on their grandparents' farm had filled the brothers with endless adventures of body and mind.

And the places their imaginations carried them!

One day, their castle of bales protected them from fire-breathing dragons; the next, they played a game of hide-and-seek on the world's largest mountain. And when truly daring, they climbed to the rafters and balanced as tightrope walkers in the circus then plunged below as paratroopers into battlefields of hay bales. A 145-acre dairy farm was truly a magical place, especially for two brothers inside Grandfather's barn.

"I guess we're trading cabernet for champagne." Private First Class Risaliti's words rose like bubbles from some deep, faraway cistern. The bubbles burst and jarred Frank, still groggy, back to reality. His eyes flickered open.

Across the aisle, a half-chewed cigar bounced from the lips of PFC Haubert. "Ya know...we've been bombin' 'em since April."

"Yeah, we've been knocking the hell out of them up 'n' down the coastline." Risaliti's wiry fingers combed through thinning black hair. He had eyes that smiled even when his mouth did not.

"'Specially last week. Air operations shoulda soften'd all key Nazi positions. Whatta ya think, Sarge?" Haubert drawled.

"Let's just hope the most important zone's been softened...the drop zone." Frank wiped the weariness from his eyes with the heels of both hands.

"Second that." Risaliti's head leaned back, and his helmet cracked against the fuselage.

"B-b-b-ob Feller...had twenty-seven wins in 1940." PFC Piero's thin lips smacked in excitement.

Frank shook his head. "Would ya take some deep breaths and relax?"

"Sorry, Sarge." Tension gathered at the edges of Piero's mouth. "I still get a little anxious before I jump." He breathed in, removed his helmet, and pushed back sweat-soaked hair with a pudgy hand.

"Hey, Sarge?" Risaliti asked. "Not to be morbid, but I read somewhere people see a light."

"What're you talking about now, Riz?"

Risaliti dropped his helmet into an open hand and stared inside. Turning it toward Frank, he showed the contents. Two black-and-white photographs pressed inside revealed a middle-aged couple and a young woman. "They say your life flashes before you. You see your birth, your family, and, in the end, there's a light."

"You're right." Frank shook his head in disgust. "That's too morbid, and something you shouldn't worry about. Focus on the mission."

He strained to see their youthful faces through the darkness but still managed an inventory of his closest friends: Risaliti, Haubert, Piero, Moore. *Just boys still.* Frank was quite aware war had a way of bonding soldiers into brothers, and these men always gave him strength to continue the fight, no matter the order, or the odds.

A Frenchman sat to his immediate right. Frank glanced at him and knew this commando was more than capable of holding his own in battle. Arthur's knowledge of the region, customs, and language would be paramount, and the reason for insertion with the Americans.

"I hear we've dropped hundreds of liddle brothas," Haubert said.

"Little what?" Arthur asked in surprisingly strong English.

Frank leaned toward his new friend. "Rubber paratroopers...hundreds of miniature rubber paratroopers dropped to confuse the Germans of our number and location."

Risaliti laughed. "No doubt, loaded like a sot trapped in a French wine cellar!"

PFC Moore, who had watched his buddies banter with a grim fascination, rolled his deep-set eyes which appeared black in the low light. "Really? That's the best you can do?"

Arthur's face twisted in confusion.

"Some of the rubber paratroopers are equipped with explosive charges...in addition to assorted firecrackers," Frank explained. "It confuses the enemy."

Haubert's tobacco-stained teeth unclenched the remnants of a cigar. "I'd love to see the look on dem Nazi bastards when they grab one! And dropped near a small town not too far from here. Riz, whatsa name of that town?"

"La Su Tat?"

"Not 'La Su Tat,' you idiot. It's pronounced La See-oh-Ta," Moore barked.

In a flash, Arthur's eyes widened and he jerked his head toward Moore. "La Ciotat?"

"Why? You heard of it?" Frank asked.

"*Oui.*" A deep frown furrowed the other man's face.

"Arthur, what's wrong?"

"I'm from La Ciotat. My family has lived there a very long time." Arthur's words rang hollow, filled with worry.

"They didn't get out?" Frank asked.

Arthur shook his head. "I know my parents. They'd never leave. I can hear my father now...something about rats leaving a sinking ship. I pray Caro's safe."

"Caro?"

"My little sister."

"But you're not sure they're still there?"

"No. I tried to send word, but the last I heard from them was two years ago. I don't know."

Frank studied his friend. Arthur tried his best to keep a poker face, but he bit his lip and his knees bounced continuously. He sensed his anxiety. But anxiety was all around him, and that was part of the job. He related quite well to it, but the gut-wrenching feeling of leaving a family behind, and the uncertainty, the inability to find out any information, and have it linger for two years? It would drive any soldier crazy.

"My mother and father were born there, like their parents before them. They refused to flee because they felt it more important to gather intelligence on German presence in Southern France. They've provided key information for operations like ours."

"They're French Resistance?"

"*Oui.*" Arthur's dimpled chin dropped to the top of his parachute pack. "I'm just worried. Especially for my little sister."

"Of course." A clear mind and sense of morale for all of his soldiers was crucial. It could mean the difference between life or death. He smiled and nodded, trying to reassure his friend. "But if she's *your* sister, she'll be fine. Your family knows this country better than any Kraut. Hell, that's why you're here, with us."

Arthur's lips eased into a smile though he remained silent.

"We're here to make it right. To help you get your homeland back."

In an instant, a red flash illuminated the men's faces, and any daydreaming ended. Jolted to reality, they prepared for battle.

"Stand and hook up!" the jumpmaster barked from the front of the fuselage. "*Ready?*"

Frank flexed his stiff shoulders and struggled to his feet. He reached above and hooked sixteen feet of static line to the cable that ran down the middle of the plane. Every man checked his helmet strap and equipment repeatedly to assure everything was secured. The last thing they wanted was anything ripped off when jumping into a plane's slipstream. He examined Arthur's gear then tapped him two times on the back reassuringly, and the process was repeated throughout the plane.

Waiting in the back of the line to leap out of a C-47 was not a big deal to Frank, but carrying a weighted pack of some 150 pounds strapped to one's body and walking down the aisle of a bouncing plane could be tricky. He felt more like an elephant lumbering through a tight, unlit tunnel than a paratrooper preparing to jump.

A green light flashed, and the line of troopers pushed forward. A right-hand turn and *Geronimo*!

Planes and parachutes filled the sky. Frank's opened with a tremendous thump, and, while the sensation of floating comforted, total blackness provided a lonely journey into an abyss. Above his head, the roar of departing plane engines slipped into nothingness. He drew a deep breath in an effort to slow his world, but the wind hissed through his form, and adrenaline coursed through him as it always did during any mission.

Enjoy the ride, soldier, but just in case... He whispered a quick prayer and scanned the world beneath his boots.

Closer to the ground, spasmodic gunfire rang. As weapons fired, flashes of light streaked like shooting stars from the barrels below. It let him know the enemy, and the ground, neared.

Pointing his toes slightly downward, he flexed his knees. Then, without warning, a loud *thud* and every bone in his body jarred to life. Both legs burned as if on fire. He wriggled his limbs until satisfied nothing important had broken.

Welcome to Le Muy, France...and to war. He ripped the first two buckles off the reserve, then the belly band and then the main parachute harness. The troopers' mantra of "secure and defend" rang in Frank's brain. He assembled his rifle and pulled out a compass. After slinging the rifle around his shoulder, he started jogging, drawing a mental line northwest.

He had lucked into an open spot for his landing and immediately searched for his buddies. But just as important—where was the enemy? Despite the lack of light, he found a large tree and leaned against it. "Apparently"—he scoured the perimeter looking for familiar landmarks—"we missed the drop zone. *Marvelous.*"

"Psst."

Frank's senses fired on all points. Falling to one knee, he flicked his 45 ACP 1911 from its holster. A leaf tumbled past his face.

"Psst."

It was a muffled sound that seemed to descend through the tree boughs. Another leaf danced past. Heart pounding, Frank scanned the inky surroundings, gun ready. Again, a ruffling as if a sudden gust of wind shook the leaves above him. But there was no breeze.

"Up *here.*"

The unmistakable form of a parachute materialized like a giant halo among the branches of the tree he leaned against.

A hushed voice cracked with emotion. "Sarge! It's me. Z."

"Private Piero?" At first, frustration filled Frank's thoughts. The need to find all his men and stay on the move was paramount. This would delay both.

"Uh-huh. I'm up crap's creek, Sarge."

But the resignation that all paratroopers faced this same dilemma with every jump reminded Frank of the obvious. *It could have happened to me.*

Piero dangled from a branch, suspended by his harness some fifteen feet above the ground. "G-g-get me out of here!"

Frank did not waste a second more. Holstering his pistol, he scanned the thick tree trunk. Three feet from the ground, a snakelike branch jutted from it, providing a foothold to climb. "Keep quiet. Just hang on."

"What?"

"Shad up! You wanna Kraut to hear?"

Within five minutes of freeing Piero, Frank spotted another friendly face. Before long, one more found his way, and then another, making a quintet of soldiers.

Moore removed his M1 helmet and cleared his throat. “Nothing seems the same as the maps we studied earlier.”

“How we gonna find the rally point now?” Risaliti dropped his head forward, allowing his helmet to fall into the palm of his open hand.

Frank stepped to the lead. “Stay together. Let’s head northwest. Move out.”

The men wound their way through the thin layer of fog blanketing the French countryside. As they walked a hedgerow, a spasm of gunfire rang in the distance. Frank raised his weapon reflexively and sank to the ground. Suddenly, foreign voices sounded on the other side of the hedge.

“Are those Frenchies or Krauts?” Piero whispered.

A distinctive West Virginian drawl rolled quietly from behind. “We need ta find Artha.”

“I can’t tell who they are,” Frank mumbled as he fingered the trigger of his rifle. “Let’s double back.”

The men staggered under the weight of their overloads and around the voices. They threaded through several small gardens and large farms, around one dead cow, near a small flock of chickens, and past a solitary horse grazing in a field of tall grass.

“Sarge, stop! Stop!”

Frank’s arm flew into a right angle, fist closed. “All stop! Piero, what’s wrong?”

“*I think*...I think we’re in a minefield!”

“Ahhh, shit!” Risaliti froze.

Private Moore’s sarcasm echoed clearly. “Well, *this* could ruin our morning.”

“Piero!” Frank’s mind raced, for time was against him. But getting out of a minefield alive could never be rushed. “How do ya know? Did you *feel* something?”

“N-n-nooo.”

Frank inhaled deeply to steady his thumping chest and sound calm. “Did you *hear* something?”

Uncertainty rang in Piero’s voice. “Not really.”

“So *why* do ya think we’re in a minefield?”

“Look...next to my b-b-boot.”

The attention of every soldier flashed to the ground.

Haubert’s twangy answer burst. “I don’t see nothin’!”

“There!” Moore’s said. “I see it, and *something*...over here.”

“Here, too!” Piero rubbed the back of his neck. “Oh man! I r-r-really don’t need this!”

“Guys, shut up! Stay focused.” Frank drew a breath and scanned the mud under his feet then spotted something to the right. “All right. I see one...hold on.” He bent his knees and distributed weight evenly between his feet. The soles of his boots dug into the ground, and his heart pounded. He forced his body lower. Lower.

“Careful, Sarge.” A nervous laugh escaped Haubert. “Man, I’m sweatin’ like a harlot in church.”

Moore chided, “Would ya shut up!”

Frank’s leg muscles throbbed; his knees strained. Closer. Closer. What at first looked disc-like now seemed round and light in color. *What in the world?* He reached out as though to caress an eggshell. His fingertips slipped over a semi-rough texture, and a faint, sweet odor rose. A familiar smell that reminded him of...Grandfather’s farm.

A wire extended from the object and ran a small length away to the others of varying size. *That’s not a wire.* Frank exhaled and his entire body relaxed. “You’ve *got* to be kidding me.” He pinched the object off the vine.

“Wha-wha-what?” Piero stammered. “S-s-sarge? What is it?”

"Hey, Piero!" Frank tossed the spherical object, slightly larger than a softball, at the private. "Catch. Melon in the hole."

"*What*? Are you crazy?" Terror filled his eyes, but Piero instinctively snatched the fruit in midair. "You trying to kill me?" he barked.

"I'm not trying to kill you. It's a melon."

"A what?" Risaliti repeated.

"A melon! We're in a *melon* field...not a minefield." Frank shook his head and continued the march. "Come on. Let's find the others."

The men exhaled and filed past Piero, who still held the fruit.

"Nice." Moore patted him on the shoulder. "Nice job, Z."

"You idiot," Haubert chuckled. "I 'bout shite myself. Thanks for nothin'!"

Under the weight of their packs, Frank and the line of soldiers snaked northwest. After wading a ravine and sliding over a small wall of rocks, they maneuvered past two more farms and arrived at a large clearing. Dawn's fog dissipated, and a meadow, almost a mile wide, lay before them. A heavily wooded area rested just beyond the field.

PFC Moore's voice perked up. "Sarge, I think that's it, the rallying point."

When they arrived, Frank discovered a large group of Americans huddled in a woodland of poplars and pines—the rest of their outfit. Weaving through the men, he caught sight of Arthur.

The Frenchman's face brightened. "*Bonjour, Frank.*"

Frank smirked. "We could've used you about an hour ago."

"Pardon, but I had my own issues."

"What happened?"

"Landed on a farmhouse and went through the roof. Let's say, I startled a family of countrymen."

"Well, the important thing is ya made it." Frank threw his shoulders back, readjusting the burden on his back.

"They offered me breakfast, the family inside."

"They're happy to know you're fighting for them."

Arthur nodded. "And I'm happy to know you're fighting for us."

Frank clasped his shoulder. "We're not fighting for you. We're fighting *with* you. Now, let's go about this business of getting your homeland back."

The commando peered at the cloudy horizon, his eyes never wavering. Dawn's rosy fingers stretched across the eastern sky, and the last of the stars flickered down like lonely children.

"Smells like pine," Frank muttered.

Arthur breathed in and grinned. His voice cracked with emotion. "Smells like home."

FOUR
God's Country

France

Lieutenant Hanz Lambrecht raised his immaculate black boots to the desktop, crossed his legs, and leaned into the creaky, wooden chair. A dull ache resonated from his lower back, the product of too much time sitting behind a desk. Arms and chest once corded with muscle ached for a return to the activity his body craved. He hoped for the winding springtime hikes on the fragrant slopes of Liechtenstein. He yearned for the wintry rush of snow under his skis. He longed for home.

Hanz wiped his stubbled face with both hands, as if weariness could be rubbed away. Fingertips pressed into the same wrinkle his father had between his eyebrows.

This war is taking its toll on me.

The *Amerikaners* had invaded the southern French coastline just twenty-four hours ago, not far from where he currently sat in Aubagne. Already, a buzz of retreat circulated in his office.

Retreat.

The word stuck in his thoughts.

In front of him lay folders and papers scattered around a half-empty bottle of cognac. A worn leather duffel bag sat to his left, and a black-and-white photograph huddled inside a handmade wooden frame lay to the right. His hands dropped to his lap and he caught sight of the family photograph.

Extending his arm, he brushed a finger over the frame with subtle reverence. Snatching a glass next to the frame, he swirled the liquid and sipped.

As a boy, Hanz had heard the story many times and understood it well. After the Great War, his parents had taken their children and fled the hustle and bustle of Munich, and in the spring of 1920, had found their way to the hidden treasure known as Liechtenstein. There, they would raise Hanz, Leisel, and Emma.

Upon arrival, teenage Hanz had embraced his new life. A passion to read and listen allowed him to quickly become fluent in various German dialects surrounding his village, as well as in French and Italian. In addition to the mental demands of school, he excelled at everything physical. He'd climbed slopes like a mountain goat, skied and swam with the fastest men, and, like a nomad, camped in the mountains for weeks at a time. When he reached his seventeenth birthday, he managed—on a dare—to ski the steepest slope of Malbun without poles.

That same night, at Geisen Haus Tavern, he pursued the affection of his childhood, Anna, only to trip over a barstool while telling a joke and drinking a stein of beer. Falling headfirst into the corner of the counter, he'd shattered his mug. A small gash above his left eye and a large dose of embarrassment were his reward. But he'd also procured a date with Anna for the following night. Shortly after, he had married his sweetheart and earned a professorship at the university, where he'd studied medicine and world history. Their daughter, Frances, was born within the first year.

He shook his head and tried to return from far away, but the past still called.

Frances had celebrated her eleventh birthday two weeks earlier. *I was not there...again. I'm so sorry, Daughter, so sorry. And my little William...only six and no father to guide him.*

His mind slipped, and in an instant, he saw Mother baking and smelled the latest batch of apple pie and strudel in the oven.

During the last few days leading to their departure, Mother cooked more than ever. A not-so-subtle attempt to keep her mind busy with work.

Liechtenstein
Winter of 1938

Hanz reread the telegram one last time. *Typical Berlin clarity and conciseness*. Despite Liechtenstein's neutrality in World War II, certain overtures were made quite clear by German command. The proposal was simple—both Lambrecht men must report to Berlin...immediately. He stood behind the kitchen table, watching his mother bake. He searched for the right words. After all, it was not every day sons and their fathers left home for war.

Despite arthritic fingers, she pulled a tray of apple pies from the oven. Mother's hands never ceased. Amazingly, it was as if working in the kitchen gave her matronly form a kind of boundless energy and strength women half her age would be jealous of. The kitchen floor, he figured, was her Antaeus. She tugged a single cooking mitt off and dipped one crooked finger into the side of a pie.

Hanz let out a long breath he hadn't realized he was holding in and swallowed to moisten his dry mouth. "Using your magic pinky, Mother?"

She smirked. "You know my thermometer."

"I know your baking." Folding the little piece of paper, he slipped it into his pants pocket and stretched for the nearby pie with his own finger, but she pulled it out of reach and winked. "Everyone in the village knows quite well...your cooking is truly a slice of heaven. You are aware everyone refers to your kitchen as *Kutchen Himmel*?"

Pushing the tray back into the oven, she peeked at him out of the corner of her eye. "*Danke*, my son.

Remember, even in the smallest of tasks, always strive for perfection."

As the aroma of pastry and pie wafted in the air, Eva wiped her hand onto an already-stained cooking apron. "Bread is God's food. But pies? Pies are for angels...*when* they are ready."

"Yes, Mother." A sly smile crossed his lips. "Where's Father?"

"In his shop, working on something special."

He admired how his father enjoyed the quiet and deep concentration of being a cobbler. Perhaps, after the atrocities of the Great War, it was needed.

Captain William Lambrecht had served Germany in the First World War before returning home. Hanz could always find his dad working late inside his workshop. One night, when much younger, Hanz spied through the open door of his shop. His father hunched over the workbench, fingering a stash of medals and ribbons Hanz had never seen before. His dad said nothing, just frowned. Father's head revolved to the entrance and he stared at Hanz. Dropping the trophies into a wooden box, he stood on a chair and shoved the box amongst the cottage rafters of his workshop.

Hanz questioned him about war.

William stepped down and explained, "When a soldier returns from war, he returns with scars. Some are visible, but the worst ones, my dear son...are not."

Any tale of war remained buried in the box and trenches in which he had fought.

Hanz wrapped both arms around his mother's shoulders, leaned in, and kissed her ruddy cheek. "Thank you, Mother, for everything. I'll never forget all you've taught."

Tears welled in Eva's eyes as she clutched her only son, her warm breath caressing his cheek. With a sniffle, she broke the embrace and spun toward the oven. "I don't want them to burn."

He focused on her form as if taking a mental snapshot. Lazy blonde curls, streaked with dashes of gray, nipped the top of her shoulder blades. Her body trembled and, even with her back to him, he knew she wept. Silhouetted by trays of pastry, she continued to work in the shimmering heat of the oven.

Finally, she turned and her quavering voice broke the silence. "Please, my son, return to me." Tears trickled down her cheeks, and he gently wiped them away. She peered into her son's face and repeated, "Whatever it takes, return to me. *Please.*"

"I will, Mother."

"My Hanz, *my* angel. May God be with you." They embraced one final time. "Always seek the light of Liechtenstein."

"I will, Mother. I promise."

Stepping from the kitchen, he looked back over his shoulder, and it struck him—*I may never see my mother again.* Somewhere deep in his soul, a hollowness reverberated. On a deep exhale, he snatched a winter jacket hanging on a wooden peg near the door and threw it over his shoulders. He stepped outside onto a path already worn in the snow. Cold mountain air shocked his lungs as he trudged in the direction of a small building separate from the house—Father's workshop.

Halfway there, Hanz paused. The sheer scale of mountain slope to valley stole his breath.

And while words to describe what he witnessed spun in his mind, it also filled him with inspiration. This was the natural grandeur of God's country. *Only the power of Liechtenstein's nature could heal most any wound, be they visible or not.*

In the valley below, crystal-clear tarns reflected the surrounding Alps with an eerie duplication. Skies of deepest blue made it almost impossible to distinguish water from air. Hanz stepped toward the workshop and eyed the snow-capped mountains towering over six-thousand feet above sea level. Massive precipices of stone cradled the valley. In cold weather, the landscape had transformed white and morphed into odd shapes and forms. Skiing from place to place was the favored mode of transportation, but this trip was quite short.

He pushed the wooden door open. "*Father*?"

"Ahhh...Hanz, my boy. Come in and close the door." William swiveled in the chair and faced him.

His father tended to be analytical and objective, gathering his thoughts and the proper evidence before making the best decision possible. That characteristic had resulted in his quick ascension through Germany's military ranks. Hanz tried to imagine the demands of the First World War and delivering a family to a new land. Those trials and tribulations, he concluded, had furrowed deep wrinkles between his father's pale-blue eyes. One particular crease extended from the bridge of his nose and pressed high into the middle of his forehead, giving the appearance of perpetual concentration.

To William's right, a large gray box sat on top of a work desk. He grabbed it with both hands and pushed it toward his son. "This...is for you."

Hanz elevated his chin and stared into his father's eyes. Pride filled his heart. "*Danke, Father.*" Removing the lid, he placed it to the side of the workbench before pulling away a covering of white tissue paper. Peeling the paper back revealed a pair of knee-high, form-fitted ebony boots. He lifted one and turned it over with utmost care. "Father, these are wonderfully crafted. I don't know what to say."

"Luckily, I do. I have already been in touch with German command. While I will be stationed in Berlin, you'll be in France."

Anxieties of duty and war whirled in his stomach. "To what end?"

"Intelligence." The wrinkle furrowed into William's forehead. "Gathering information on the Maquis, the French Resistance. At least my son will not be on the front line."

A twinge of doubt seeped into his thoughts. He buried it behind a confident smile. "But that would not bother me."

William drew a labored breath and slumped his shoulders. "Why is it that when men are young, they want to die for a cause? When they are old, they want to live because of one."

"Since I am neither young nor old, or agree with the cause to begin with"—he straightened his back as if for a need of military etiquette—"what does that make me?"

"It makes you...my only son." William stood, wrapped an arm around him, and pulled him close. "Please, Hanz. Do your duty. Be honorable. Be diligent. Above all, stay safe."

Tears welled. But he blinked them away so Father wouldn't see. "I will, Father. I promise."

William cleared his throat and a renewed sense of hope filled his voice. "And if we happen to survive the conclusion of Germany's war, we'll live the rest of our years quite well with our family."

"In the light of Liechtenstein," Hanz chuckled. "We'll share many good laughs and—"

Father smiled and squeezed his arm. "And the best of cognacs—"

"And be quite content to age gracefully." Hanz leaned back and grinned. "To see my children grow."

"Your *children*?" William's jaw dropped. His lower lip trembled. "Plural?"

"Frances is going to have a sister...or brother." Hanz beamed with a surge of pride. "Anna's expecting. Doctor Huber confirmed this morning."

His dad touched his cheek and gazed at him. "It is strange. War brings out the worst of mankind, but, at the same time, reveals what is best in all men and women. Come, we must get ready."

"I know, Father. War is waiting."

William's fingers ruffled his son's hair. "Let it wait. Tonight, we celebrate new life."

Private Kurt Schmidt rapped on the open office door with enough force, the glass window of the frame rattled in its rest. With tightly-cropped blond hair pressed under his service cap, and a flawless, shining youthful face, the nineteen-year-old soldier was a portrait of the Arian race.

His tenor voice broke the lieutenant's reverie. "*Heil Hitler!*"

Hanz Lambrecht rubbed any trace of weariness from his eyes with fingers cramped from hours of writing reports. "Private?"

"The order just came through. We must pull out within the hour."

"North? To Lyon, I assume."

The young man nodded. "*Jawohl, mein Lieutenant!*"

"*Danke.*" Lambrecht pulled his boots off the desktop and stuffed the papers into their corresponding folders and then into the worn leather duffel bag. With one hand, he grasped the framed photograph and studied it for a moment.

"Sir?"

Slowly, a bit distracted by his past, Hanz slipped the treasured frame inside his leather bag. "Yes, private."

"The war?"

"What about it?"

"The importance of losing a battle?"

"Ahhh. You are concerned about losing the coast so quickly? Don't worry. Not all wars are lost with a single battle...or even battles."

Private Schmidt, with a renewed sense of pride beaming from his countenance, threw out his right arm in salute. "*Heil Hitler!*" Spinning on his heels, he strode from the office and closed the door.

And not all Germans... The words slipped from Lambrecht's lips carelessly. "Are Nazis."

He bolted down the remaining cognac from his glass and dropped it onto the desktop. Grabbing his leather case, he strode to a waiting car.

FIVE
Winter

Caro stretched out on a woolen blanket in the fields beyond La Ciotat. When she opened her eyes, a twilight sky stretched above. There were no clouds, just alternate streaks of pink and lavender. She stared.

Waiting.

Something dark and terrible must happen. For those same feelings turned inside her. And then they pressed upon her chest. A great, heavy burden seemed to settle on her like a chunk of iron. One minute passed. Then another. But nothing bad happened.

Rolling her head to the side, she faced a small cardboard box she had carried into the hills.

Empty. Like my spirit.

In a world of melancholy, it was the saddest she felt since the beginning of war. Caro closed her eyes, and, for a moment, cleared a flood of memories. German shouts, her empty stomach, the gunshots, and her parents' bloody bodies strewn on the ground. All dissipated into the afternoon sky.

But, an instant later, she remembered again, and, before she knew it, tears fell without a sound. With a sigh, she sat up and scanned the horizon in every direction. No one came. Nothing to hurt or destroy what she loved.

She ran her frayed brown sleeve across both cheeks. A gnarled thread dangled from the shirt sleeve, and she picked at it. As hard as she tried, she couldn't remember when she'd last worn new clothes.

That was before the war, another lifetime. *That world does not exist anymore.*

She'd cried herself to sleep when Arthur left, but this interminable emptiness...loneliness...was much different. This was a talon grief that refused to loosen its grip on her heart. Sharp and cutting and unbearable.

Maman.

The absolute misery consumed her soul.

Papa.

Four Years Earlier—July 1940

The fifteen-year-old bounded down the path. Her short raven hair brushed her shoulder tops as she breathed in the sweet summer air and exhaled a happy hum.

Stopping at the water's edge, she raised her hand reflexively to shield her eyes from the setting sun's glare, made especially sharp by the water's reflection.

Caro ducked around the corner of the boathouse, threw open the door, and skipped toward the ladder. She grabbed a bottom rung and climbed.

Halfway up, she paused and whispered, "Arthur?"

No response. She counted the last rungs as if playing a game. "*Trois...deux...un!*" At the top, she leaped into the loft.

The bed of straw tickled her bare knees as she crawled over it. A figure nestled in the corner came into sight. Resting on his back, he stared through a small hole in the ceiling above his head. A single ray of slanted light bathed his youthful face. An earthen tile of terracotta roof leaned against the wall.

"I knew you'd be hiding here," she giggled.

"You did?" He glanced at her and smiled.

Lying next to her eighteen-year-old brother's lanky form, she wiggled close and mimicked his posture. "What're you staring at?"

"I'm waiting for the first star."

Caro scratched her knees, itchy from the straw. "My teacher says stars are made of fire. Like candles that burn at church."

"Like candles?" Arthur laughed, his acorn-shaped eyes squinting in delight. "Then do they melt and burn out? Or do they last forever?"

"Hmmm. I don't know." She shrugged. "I never thought about that."

"Remember, Caro"—Arthur raised his arm and pointed to the aperture, the twilight sky beyond—"even in the darkest night, there's light. And light always seeks light." The smile on his face flattened, and his voice lowered in tone. "You know I leave tonight?"

"*Oui.*" At the thought of losing Arthur, her throat tightened around the words. "I know."

"I may not see you..." A deep breath escaped him. "For a very long time."

A tear trickled onto her cheek and rolled from her face, unchecked.

"Now don't cry. I have something for you." His hand disappeared into a pants pocket. "Close your eyes."

She obeyed.

"Open your hand." Cold metal links piled into the cup of her palm. "Okay. You can look."

Her voice raised with excitement. "Where'd you get this?"

"I traded for it."

"Arthur, it's beautiful!" Caro sat up and threw her arms around him tight, refusing to let go, not knowing the next time she would see him. Then, resting her head on his chest, she listened to his heartbeat and lost herself in its rhythm.

"Caro." Her brother paused. "I can stay no longer."

Her head slumped to Arthur's side. A strand of hair slipped onto her face, and he brushed it away with a tender touch.

"I'm old enough now and have to join the fight like *Papa et Maman*."

"But why?"

"They say the Germans will never leave, and someday, when the time is right, we must make them."

They lay side by side, their breathing almost one.

"Caro, there may come a day when you are very scared, and, if that time comes, promise me you'll be brave." Arthur leaned on one elbow and stared into her face.

Despite the pale light, she saw him clearly. Her brother's long-lashed dark eyes reminded her of *Maman's*. His smooth, fair skin reminded her of the flour in Aunt Margaret's bakery.

"You must do whatever it takes...to endure...to survive...to carry on what *Papa et Maman* have started. Promise me."

"But *they* will know what to do! Won't they?"

"Promise me."

She didn't know exactly what he asked, but she nodded. "I promise." Her fingers folded around Arthur's strong, callused hands and squeezed. "And you?"

"Training first. Fighting next."

Caro gazed at the shiny locket. "It's *magnifique*." And any sister could interpret his rosy blushed response—*you're welcome.*

"I'm glad you like it. I traded for it. Four good fish." He paused. "No matter what, sister, I'll always be with you. I'll always be here." His fingertip pointed to her heart. "Open the locket."

Pinching the clasp open, she exposed the tiny silver case. A favorite family picture lay tucked inside.

He leaned close, his warm breath tickling her ear. "I'm going to miss my Caro."

"Arthur, this is *wonderful*! And I'm...I'm going to miss you as well," she said softly.

"Miss your brother? I never imagined." With a smirk, he tilted his head toward the overhead opening. "Look, Caro! There it is."

"What?"

"*La première étoile de la nuit!*" The first star of the night!

Arthur draped his arm around her shoulder and drew her into his embrace. The warmth of his body comforted her and, for a moment, everything seemed right with the world. Time stood still as she stared at the heavenly light. Finally, she blurted. "*When*? When will I see you again?"

Arthur breathed deeply, his words as distant as the star they stared at. "I don't know. I just don't know."

Their mother's voice, though faint, echoed through the hole in the roof. "Caroline! Come to the house!"

"You must go—now," Arthur whispered.

Caro clutched her brother even tighter and sniffled.

"Here." He leaned back, snatched the locket from her hand, and fastened it around her neck.

The cool metal links blinked against the moonlight. "Can't you stay here, with me...*forever*?" She wiped her nose with the back of her hand and sniffled again.

"*Non*. I can't. I can't hide here any longer. It's too dangerous."

Giving Arthur one last, sad look, she pulled away and reached for the ladder top, but her hand froze in midair. "I *know*, I just—"

"Caro, remember..." Her teary eyes searched his face, and he continued, "The light...be like the stars and moon. Always run to light. Always. Now, go. *Maman* is calling."

Not wanting to leave her brother's side, she climbed slowly down the ladder and dragged her feet along the path. While her spirit felt light after having spent precious time with Arthur, the closer her small steps carried her to home, the stronger a feeling of dread weighed upon her. Perhaps it had been the tone of her mother's voice when she'd called out moments ago. Maybe because she had been told, many times, that the war had created a different world, even in places like La Ciotat, and everyone should be wary, especially a fifteen-year-old girl. An alarming quiet enveloped the land around her, forcing her gaze back to the tranquil coastline. Then, as Caro continued around the last bend of path and a final cluster of palm trees, she glanced at the house and gasped.

Her heart sank into her stomach.

A German soldier stood at rigid attention, guarding the entrance. Her strides shrank as she approached. He was the largest man she had ever seen.

Though *Maman* had warned her to never stare at the enemy, she couldn't help herself. As discreetly as possible, she searched his face, hoping for a clue to his thoughts or intentions. But his stern, unflinching countenance stared forward as if chiseled of stone. He neither blinked nor acknowledged her existence with any movement. Slipping past, she rushed through the opened door and into the kitchen.

Caro stopped, frozen in place.

Another soldier in a pristine German uniform sat at the kitchen table. Compared to his fierce counterpart outside, he sat, relaxed, his chair pushed away from the wooden table at a slight angle, allowing his legs to cross. A peaked officer's cap perched on his lap, and his right arm rested on the tabletop, his fingertips clicking rhythmically. In the center of the table, a slim white candle, its flame flickering on the walls, burned atop a wine bottle, a postcard of La Ciotat and its mountainous sentinel propped against it.

A half-filled glass of rosé and a plate of sliced Etorki cheese rested next to the man's elbow. Mother sat to his right. To those who knew her well, the smile she wore was more forced than natural as she calmly turned an empty glass in her hands. Caro's father cut a loaf of fresh bread at the counter.

Though Caro felt as if her chest would burst with fear, she noticed how calmly and patiently Father moved.

"I have to admit, though, I don't like it." The officer's flawless French had a harsh tone, perhaps more than he intended. "You people surely have your secrets."

Unsure what to think, Caro silently rehearsed her parents' instructions when dealing with any German. Speak when spoken to, be respectful, *and remember our story*.

Father turned, faced the man, and smiled, offering him a generous slice of warm baguette her mother had baked that morning. "It's good to see you again, Lieutenant Lambrecht."

The officer accepted it with a grin. "Tell me how you French manage to do it?"

"Do what?" Papa asked.

"Make the finest bread in Europe." He nibbled on a corner then placed the slice on his plate.

"I believe, Lieutenant, the secret is in the flour and yeast." Papa walked to the sink and rinsed the blade. "And patience." The knife in his hand stilled. "You cannot rush a good bread."

"Or a good wine." The German chuckled. Thrusting his glass into the air, almost in salute, he downed the remaining contents with one quick gulp.

Caro studied him, memorizing everything about him. He had a tiny silver scar on his forehead, just above his left eyebrow, and his close-cropped blond hair had patches of gray at the temples. His black boots were immaculately polished, and he did not wear a weapon. And he was not nearly as big as the soldier outside. Turning in her direction, he smiled. It spread across his face, disarming her.

"Ahhh. And who is this sweet darling?"

Maman's eyes jerked wide for an instant, but her features softened as she replied, "Our daughter Caroline. She was with her aunt when last you visited."

"Caroline! What a pretty name. And her eyes! The violet eyes of an angel." A hand extended in her direction. "Come here, child."

She stepped forward, and the German placed a hand on her shoulder. Her eyes darted to *Maman et Papa*. Both faces expressed a calm facade, yet a twinge of discernable concern ticked from the corners of their mouths.

Always concern.

Shifting nervously in her chair, her mother blurted, "She's only eleven."

Caro played along with the bluff and nodded.

"Only eleven?" The officer grinned again then pulled a glossed-leather satchel from under the table and opened a pouch. "Would you believe I have a daughter who lives in Liechtenstein?"

Caro's body was rooted to the floor.

"*She* is also eleven..." His eyes found her father's, and he winked. "But much smaller than your lovely daughter." The chain around Caro's neck sparkled with rays of light, and, distracted, he fingered the silver links. "And look! What a lovely locket!"

Too frightened to move, Caro stared at the scar above his eyebrow and whispered, "*Merci*."

Lambrecht's hand groped inside the pouch and pulled out a small, stuffed bear, dangling it before her. "A surprise for the lovely Caroline."

Her gaze dropped to his immaculate boots. "But I...I have no money."

"Hmmm. No money. Tsk, tsk, tsk." He withdrew his hand and the bear. "What to do...what to do? Any ideas?"

She shook her head.

"I have it!" He punctuated the air with his fingertip. "What is your favorite song?"

"My favorite song?" Puzzled at the unexpected question, she bit her lip.

He nodded. "*Oui.*"

The softest of responses escaped her lips. "'Au Clair de la Lune.'"

"Well, if you sing for me, I will accept that as payment." He waggled the bear to tempt her.

Glancing toward her parents, she searched their faces for permission. Papa nodded.

Caroline tugged her shirt, stood tall in front of the German, and lowered her gaze to the wooden floor. She summoned a voice deep within her being. It carried all of the fear, hope, and love she felt for her family at that very moment.

Lambrecht's eyes widened, and the giant guard outside, who had neither blinked nor moved, poked his head through the doorway and into the kitchen.

In the moonlight,
My friend Pierrot,
Lend me your quill
To write a word...

The lieutenant's shoulders softened then his attention turned to the table. He stretched for the postcard leaning against the wine bottle and flipped it over. Tapping the card against the tabletop, he stared as if examining it. He eased into the chair, tilted his head back, and closed his eyes, rubbing the stamp under his thumb in a slow, methodical rhythm.

Mama's glare met Papa's. Caro continued, her voice resonating throughout the house,

By the light of the moon
Likeable Lubin
Knocks on the brunette's door.

With all that looking
I don't know what was found,
But I do know that the door
Shut itself on them.

A hushed silence hung in the air.

His eyes flickered open as if waking from the most pleasant of dreams. Lambrecht exhaled deeply. "*Magnifique.*" He blinked, and a smile lit his face. "Simply *magnifique.*" With a rapid but measured movement, he propped the postcard against the wine bottle again. Then, as if remembering the need for military protocol, he straightened his shoulders, rose, and grabbed the satchel. "Take care of your family, Charles, and always remember...we are never far."

Then, he extended his hand and cupped Caro's chin. With piercing blue eyes, he studied her face as if searching for something familiar. "An angel. *This,* my dear, is for you." The bear fell into her small hands. "Simply *magnifique.*" Lambrecht spun away and strode from the room.

Out in the yard, the car engine roared to life then slowly disappeared over a rise and into the night.

Her father ran to the doorway and peered outside before turning back and facing his family. A look of relief washed across his face in such a way that Caro had never seen. He dropped to one knee and beckoned. Reaching out, Charles clutched his wife and daughter and clung to them.

August 1944

Caro stood and sighed. She gathered the blanket and grabbed the empty box. Before long, her footsteps led her to town and toward her aunt and uncle's bakery.

As her heels clicked on the cobblestone road, she peered into the sky. A final blade of orange sunlight cut across building tops, causing long shadows to droop onto the side of road she walked. It seemed the darkness knew her every step, determined to cover her very being.

She entered the bakery.

But the usual aroma of freshly baked bread that greeted her was absent. Except for a candlelight flickering in the back room near the ovens, blackness enveloped the kitchen. No baking today...again.

"*Tante?*" Caro pulled the door closed behind her. "*Oncle?*" She looked to her left. Two immaculate aprons hung from wooden pegs near the door.

Her uncle's gruff voice echoed from the rear of the store. "Caro?" Uncle Jean's wide form shuffled forward past the empty display cases.

"Is everything okay?" he huffed, short of breath.

She nodded. "*Oui.*"

A deep exhale escaped his lips. His head lowered, almost in defeat, then his arm slipped under hers, and he led her to a table in the back room. Usually, warmth from the ovens pressed against her skin. Tonight, a silence and stillness hung in the room, sparking an unnerving chill along her spine.

"Sit, my dear."

She slipped into the chair he pulled out for her, and he plopped on one next to her.

Light danced on the walls as she slid the empty box over the tabletop next to the candle.

She searched her uncle's face for a strength she currently lacked. The pale candlelight allowed her to trace the shape and color of his eyes. *How much like Papa*. But despite the recent tragedy of losing his brother, determination and strength set in the lines around his mouth and cheeks.

All the way there, she had planned what she would say, but when she saw her father's eyes in his brother's face, she faltered.

"I am scared," she blurted at last.

Jean flashed a tender smile. "As we all are. As we all *must* be." Stretching his hands across the table, he gave hers a light squeeze. "But..." Something glittered in his expression. "That does not make us helpless."

Caro sat in silence, trying to conjure a sentence to describe what turned in her heart. It eluded her. She stared at her uncle.

His face ended in a blunt chin that immediately gave way to a fleshy roll of neck. A heavy man before the war, he'd lost considerable weight since. Yet, he and Aunt Margaret were still built like the loaves of boule they sometimes baked.

"There were no *cigales* in the hills today," she said, her voice low. "My box is empty."

"The cicadas will return, child, like many things, when this war ends."

"Will they?" she asked. "And what of life then?"

Jean sighed. "War makes us doubt...everything."

"I am beginning to doubt life itself."

"Caro..." *Oncle* gazed at her, parental affection gleaming in his eyes. "Though we doubt, there are some things we should never question." His weight shifted in the chair. "Never doubt your family's love. Never doubt your French heritage. Never doubt the importance of your parents' efforts. But right now, at this moment, never doubt the flame of French Resistance. It must not die."

She nodded, and something deep inside her sparked to life. She welcomed it.

"We have all felt Nazi brutality. Columns of German soldiers. Hordes of displaced French citizens. And what has been done to *anyone* of Jewish descent is beyond comprehension. If we have learned anything from this terrible war, it is that we cannot be silent."

"I know," she whispered. "I just miss them. I miss them terribly."

"As do I."

"How do you do it?" she asked. "How do you go on despite the death and darkness?"

"I go on, as *you* will. One day at a time." The lines of determination in his face tightened. "You, my dear, are stronger than you ever believed, and *you* must see it."

To that, she had no response.

"You were impetuous in your youth. *Sneaking* my cookies as a child," he teased.

A twinge of a smile tugged at her lips.

"And while war seems to break all of us, the very good and very righteous..." He focused on the ovens and became still. "It can also make us stronger, especially in the places we *think* are broken."

Caro exhaled. "I will try," she said at last. "I will finish the work *Papa* and *Maman* started. I know their ways."

"And *you*, my dear niece, are a wonder."

She wiped her cheek with the frayed sleeve, a habit from so much crying. She looked at her uncle as the words spilled from her mouth. "I...I have no more tears."

Cupping her chin, he raised it and studied her eyes. "No more tears. But plenty of French resolve."

A bone-deep fatigue gnawed at her soul, but something surged in the same chest that suffered moments ago as if a great weight lay upon it.

"You have postcards? Pyramidon?" he asked.

"*Oui.* Everything I need to write in our special ink."

"Then, we continue our efforts. Our scouts will contact us soon." As he pushed the chair away with the back of his legs and stood, a slight groan escaped his lips. "My back is not what it once was," he said. "But, come. We must get home. Your *tante* is most certainly wondering why cleaning a floor has taken so long." With a quick breath, he leaned forward and blew out the candle.

She followed him into the next room and out of the bakery. As she stood on the cobblestone street and waited for him to lock the door, she shivered in the cold night air. Clutching the collar of her drab, brown shirt, she pulled it tight around her neck.

He turned and faced her. "Ready?"

Caro nodded. "*Merci, Oncle...*for everything."

"Remember, my dear, war is winter, but the promise of spring never fails." Uncle Jean repeated his last words, singing gleefully. *"The promise of spring never fails. And we must never be silent."* His cheeks were blotchy red as a chuckle escaped his lips. "Now, come. Aunt Margaret has prepared dinner. Spend the night." Reaching for her hand, he pulled her near. "Rest. Gather your strength. For tomorrow is a new day."

She glanced over her shoulder at the bakery entrance. "Wait. I forgot my box."

"Leave it," he said. "Tomorrow we fill it with bread."

SIX
Homecoming

The efficiency of the war machine known as the American military still amazed Sergeant Frank Taylor. The ability to move a hundred thousand soldiers and countless tons of equipment, and do it with resourceful precision, would be the envy of every country by the end of the war. Like an endless swarm of bees, American troops never ceased. And before long, its accomplishments were breathtaking and, in many instances, for the enemy, devastating.

With Le Muy liberated and its perimeter secured, the soldiers established camp in a hive of activity. Tents, halls, hospitals, and headquarters sprang to life. Frank strolled to the mess hall and pondered their latest order. Tasked with "shielding arriving supplies" from any sort of German counter, he understood the command as a veiled effort for a well-deserved seventy-two-hour respite for his unit, and he welcomed the break. The Germans were on the run, and everyone knew it.

As Frank waited in line, the unfamiliar aroma of powdered eggs and bacon wafted through the cool morning air. The smell reassured him something as normal as breakfast did not have to be dried or opened in a can. Relaxed chow time meant the opportunity to share meals and stories with his men. The brief moments of downtime helped bond them into an efficient team. Carrying a mess kit at his hip with one hand and a cup of black coffee with the other, he noticed Arthur sat separately from most of the men. Frank ambled to his table.

"*Bonjour*, Arthur."

The Frenchman glanced up. "Frank, *bonjour*. Sit."

Sliding over the bench, he patted the space next to him as a husky voice shouted from a nearby table, "Hey, Sarge?"

Frank squinted at the slick-haired soldier. "What do you need, Martinez?"

"Who's betta, the Indians or Yankees?" Martinez cocked his head as if he already knew the answer.

"I know you're from the Bronx, but, the last time I checked...the Indians."

Martinez's shoulders wilted in displeasure and he waved a dismissive hand.

Frank plopped onto the seat and admired his hot plate of food on a deep inhale. "At least you didn't have to crash through a roof to get chow this morning."

Arthur gave him a weak smile while he rolled his fork between the eggs and bacon, playing with it.

"You look sad," Frank blurted.

Arthur sighed. "That obvious?"

It reminded Frank how similar they were. Like all soldiers, they were far from home and away from loved ones. He wanted to comfort him but hesitated. "Thinking of your family?"

Arthur lowered his fork and nodded. "*Oui.*"

"When's the last time you saw them?"

"I last *saw* them four years ago." Arthur blinked, bleary-eyed. "I last *heard* from them nine months ago." He reached into his jacket, pulled out a postcard, and handed it to Frank. The picture on the front revealed small houses, docks, and boats of all color nestled near a bay, with a hunchback of rock surrounding a village.

"Arthur, it's beautiful." He patted him on the shoulder.

"*Merci...*" Arthur whispered. "And it's home."

Frank turned the postcard over, revealing a name, address, and short message written in French. "*Tante Sissel*?"

"My parents wrote to 'Aunt' Sissel when they had information to deliver. The first three letters, 'Sis,' is code for the British Foreign Intelligence Organization...formally known as the 'Secret Intelligence Service.' ...SIS."

With a raised eyebrow, Frank considered the idea of delivering secret information to a fictitious aunt whose first three initials were an acronym for an intelligence agency. "You're kidding me."

"A Frenchman never kids about espionage."

"What does the message say?"

Arthur's expression turned thoughtful. "The one you can see? Nothing more than '*We miss you. Hope all is well. Look forward to your next visit. Love, Charles and Anne.* Charles and Anne are my father and mother.

"But I don't see any *secret* information. It's from your family, right?"

"First, it is my mother's hand. Our handler, after receiving it in England, passed it to me as a courtesy. Look carefully."

"I still don't—" Then Frank found it. An almost microscopic manuscript rested at the very spot a stamp once sat. He strained to read the two-column message. Each column contained four words, making a total of eight. "And this says?"

"*Tell Arthur. Stay safe. Family Fine. Love you.* What you *can* see is the message I just read, once hidden under the stamp. What you *can't* see is the message containing Nazi troop position, movement, ammo dumps, and radar installations between the lines you *can* see. My parents learned to use an invisible ink. It's made by dissolving a tablet of pyramidon in white gin. Pyramidon is a common treatment for headache."

"Well, I'll be..." Frank groped for a word to express his surprise.

Arthur's gaze settled on the postcard. "In war, one must learn to read between the lines."

"Literally."

"*Oui.* To defeat the enemy, you have to know where he is." He paused as Frank handed the card back. "The more exact, the easier it is."

"And the address? How'd you get it?"

"Postcards travel to Marseille by boat...local fishermen. From there, to a courier known as the Fly. They deliver to French government exiled in England, also by boat. And from there, to M16, or as we say with affection, Aunt Sissel. After reporting the information, our handler delivered it to me. I was in England preparing for the invasion, before training with you."

Frank shook his head in amazement.

"My parents supplied much information over the years." Arthur rubbed the postcard with his thumb then inserted it carefully into his breast pocket. "I miss them. I miss them terribly."

"Arthur..." A thought entered Frank's mind then opened and filled him with excitement. "What's the distance from La Ciotat to our position?"

"By automobile...a little more than an hour's drive. It's west, along the coast."

The moment he heard the answer, Frank had a reply that surprised even him. "How'd you like to go there? For a *brief* visit?"

"Home?" Arthur's eyes shot wide.

"Yep."

Leaning in, Arthur whispered, "Can we do that?"

With the plan still rolling in Frank's mind, he spoke quietly. "We have a window of seventy-two hours. Our orders are to shield the beachhead before being mobilized. La Ciotat is part of the beachhead, isn't it?"

A wide smile morphed on his friend's face. "Frank, *merci!*"

"Don't thank me yet. We still have to commandeer a vehicle and *get* there. But I think I can handle that."

Arthur shifted his weight as if to stand. "When do we leave?"

"Soon. Stay seated. Finish eating."

Risaliti's voice interrupted as he shoved a piece of bacon into his mouth and strode toward the table. "Looks like meat's back on the menu, boys!"

"Show me a piece a food ya don't like," Haubert growled, trailing behind.

Privates Risaliti and Haubert plopped their mess kits onto the tabletop. Powdered eggs jumped to attention before settling back into their tins. Risaliti's knowledge of the Italian language and Haubert's fluency in German proved more than useful. Privates Piero and Moore, both expert marksmen, quickly joined.

Frank glanced at his men and bit his lip, lost in thought. All had endured boot camp, training, and the Italian campaign. *They entered as boys and, having survived, like me, emerged as men.* But he also understood they still loved to act like fun-loving kids when the opportunity presented itself.

"I guess the landin' was a *overwhelmin'* success!" Haubert's freckled face was framed by a shock of tight brown curls.

"I hear the Germans couldn't retreat fast enough." Risaliti chuckled, his eyes narrowed every time he laughed. "Not only did we defeat their counterattacks, the Nazis have started a complete withdrawal. I also hear that German units in Toulon have surrendered, and Marseille is liberated."

Haubert stopped chewing and stared at his buddy. "Well, I heard the Germans are retreatin' *throughout* Southern France. But honestly, Riz...the only thing you need to worry about is ya hairline."

Risaliti's hand zipped under his helmet. "What do ya mean?"

"It's the only thing retreatin' fasta than the Germans."

Risaliti shook his head with disdain. "That's wrong. Just wrong. Z, tell him that's wrong."

"That's wrong, Hobs...wrong, b-b-but true." Fixed in an expressionless gaze, Piero stared, as if pondering some profound thought. "Hey, Joe, ya seen my magazine?"

"What?" PFC Moore's lanky frame squeezed between Piero and Haubert on the bench, his elbows flared as if boxing out a position on a basketball court.

Piero stammered. "Y-y-ya know, with ears the size of yours, I'd figure you'd give me at least half of one. My *magazine!* The football annual!"

"Don't think I have. I'm pretty sure Hobs took it to the latrine."

"Wonderful." Piero waved his hand in disgust. "I'll never get it now."

"Ya probly don't want it." Haubert shoveled another forkful of food into an already-full mouth.

Risaliti pushed an empty tray to the center of the table. "So, Sarge, think we'll see any French beauties?"

"You wouldn't know what to do if ya found one." Moore jammed half a roll into his mouth. "But I do hear the countryside is filled with women happy to see American servicemen...*if* you know what I mean. Arthur, you know any beauties?"

Arthur's cheeks reddened. "They'll *all* be happy to see us."

"You know what'd make me happy? Fishing in one of those there rivers." Haubert reached into his shirt pocket and pulled out a half-chewed cigar.

"*I'd* like to find a case of fine red wine and take it home and get drunk with my Cat. We'd make love in an open f-f-field under the night sky," Piero sighed.

Moore's mouth flew open. "You want to get your pet inebriated and make love to it? That's the most disgusting thing I've ever—"

Piero smacked him on the back of the head. "Cat's my girlfriend, and yes, s-s-she's human. We plan on getting married after the war."

"So, I assume Cat's short for Catherine?" Risaliti asked.

"Yeah. But I like to think it's short for catastrophe. I love her to death, but she's the clumsiest person I know. That's how we met. I was standing at the bus stop when she tripped over the curb and fell into my arms." Piero smiled. "My girl f-f-fell for me, and then, I fell for her."

Frank cut into the conversation. "Guys, bring it in for a sec." The table of men huddled around. "We're not moving out for three days. Right now, it's 0800. Arthur's home is about sixty miles due west from where we're sitting. By vehicle, that's a little more than an hour. I'm thinking of getting him home to see the family he's not seen in four years. You guys good with that?"

The men bobbed their heads in agreement.

"Sarge?" Moore asked. "You think it's safe? I mean, there're still Germans floatin' around out there."

"According to the latest reports, we control everything from Marseilles to Le Muy. La Ciotat is between the two and buried along the coast. We'll be all right." The tone of certainty in his own voice reassured Frank. "Let's do this. Gentlemen, we'll return within seventy-two hours."

"Go, Sarge." Haubert gnawed a chunk of tobacco from the cigar stub in his hands. "We'll cova' for ya."

Piero's eyes widened. "Good luck."

Moore patted Arthur on the shoulder. "Wish you the best, Arthur. *Bonne chance!*"

"Take care, both you." Risaliti tilted his helmet back with his thumb.

Frank stood, his thoughts on the vehicle dilemma. Then, remembering the cooks' Class A pass allowed them to come and go without restriction, he nodded to Arthur. "Let's get our gear."

*****

Sure enough, a Jeep, fueled and ready, rested behind the makeshift kitchen. Both men slid into the vehicle, and Frank turned the ignition. The engine roared to life then the vehicle lurched forward, gears grinding. Before long, the French countryside surrounded them. Flashes of green grasses, hedgerows, and trees whizzed by, replacing the browns of dust, mud, and dirt in camp.

Frank released his breath in a sigh of relief and leaned back, their escape complete. "So, what's it like? Your hometown?"

"La Ciotat is a place where you feel nature's beauty." Arthur inhaled deeply with an expression somewhere between meditation and contentment. "God's presence is everywhere—in the blues of the water, the sands of the beach...the rolling green hills on which the village rests. Wherever you walk, it's either up or down. Winters are mild and summer is perfection. Father fishes on Sunday and catches enough to feed us for days. His favorite fishing spot is next to three steep cliffs overlooking the village on the west side of the bay. But up the coastline is a sight unlike any other. It is a rock formation called Le Bec D'Aigle...the eagle's beak. It is said that God placed it there to protect our village from calamity. Stories of old say in the beginning, the land and sea made love, and La Ciotat was born."

"The picture...on the postcard?" Frank swerved the vehicle to avoid a large hole in the road.

"Oui."

"Tell me about your family."

"Mother's eyes are quiet. And her hair is black as the richest soil. And her cooking? She grills fish and covers them with garlic and fennel. We have a coal stove with no thermostat, but she'd cook anything to perfection. What we eat and drink changes only with the seasons. Cheese, bread, fruit, wine. My father loves his wine. He puts it in soup during meals."

Frank steadied his bouncing helmet with one hand and steered around another small crater with the other.

"Our house, like most homes in town, are built on inclines. Red and white rose bushes line the front flower bed, and three stone steps lead to a porch. From there, the smell of *Maman's* cooking leads you inside to the kitchen."

"Sounds like paradise." A chuckhole jolted both the vehicle and passengers.

"It's a place where one feels all the happiness of life and nature and humanity." Arthur's body stiffened. His rigid jawline set in determination, appearing even more pronounced than usual. "But the Germans stole that..."

A thin column of black smoke wisped over the next hill. "Look!" Frank ground the gears and slowed the vehicle as the men reached for their M-1 Garand rifles. Before the crest of the hill, they screeched to a full stop. He switched the ignition off and whispered, "Listen." They strained to hear. "Anything?"

Arthur shook his head, and they jumped from the vehicle.

Scanning for any indication of danger, they slung the rifles over their shoulders and moved stealthily. Peeking over a ridge, they spied a curl of smoke emanating from a single vehicle, a scorched Nazi swastika spread across the car door's side. Other than a few birds streaking in the sky, they neither saw nor heard movement or sound from the valley before them.

"They were strafed." Frank craned his neck to the blue sky, in case any other aircraft threatened, and adjusted his sliding helmet. "We're good. Let's go."

They withdrew to the vehicle and cleared the hill. Reaching the smoldering car, Frank pressed the brake. Two German occupants, riddled with bullet holes and splattered with dried blood, lay frozen in death's embrace. The driver slumped forward on the steering wheel, his uniform charred black. The thin passenger, his bare head split open by a direct hit and mouth agape, wore an officer's jacket, his body splayed backward. For now, their grave remained the vehicle in which they lay.

Frank wondered if witnessing death would ever become easier but already knew the answer. He winced and slammed on the accelerator. "Let's get outta here."

*****

"You weren't kidding about the hills," Frank joked.

"Turn left here." Arthur's expression lit with the reflection and anticipation of home. "Four years..." His voice quieted. The Jeep zipped up and down another hill and whizzed by a variety of small shops. He pointed. "Uncle Jean and Aunt Margaret operate a bakery, there. Every day, after school, Caro and I would stop and see them. They always treated us." He chuckled. "Both are built like the loaves of boule they bake in their ovens, thick and round. I can't wait to surprise them."

They wound down one last hill, leaving the small shopping district of town. Frank frowned. "Not many people outside, are there?"

Arthur ignored the question and bit his lip. "Left...here. Follow as it curves right. Slow down. Over there!"

The vehicle whined to rest in front of a bleached white house on the bottom slope of a hill. Stepping from the vehicle, they stretched their legs.

Palm trees and shrubbery dotted the landscape green. Rows of rose bushes lined the front flower bed, having surrendered long ago to an invading force of chest-high weeds. A white-tiled porch rested above three stone steps, and the door to the house stood closed.

"Down there, around the bend"—Arthur pointed toward the bay—"sits Father's boathouse." He spun, bound up to the house and threw open the door, disappearing inside.

The beauty of La Ciotat sprawled in front of Frank. He inhaled a breath of salt-scented air and scanned the ocean stretching before him. *I could live in a place like this...for a very long time.*

Arthur emerged from darkness and yelled, "No one's here, not even my little sister. Maybe at the neighbors. Stay here. It's a short walk."

Frank strode to a wrought iron bench resting beneath an enormous poplar tree. He plopped down and stared at the lush hillside. The faint sound of waves slapped the shore somewhere below him, and the chattering of seagulls echoed above.

Removing his helmet, he placed it on his lap. The sun's warmth pressed the top of his head and arms. *Can it be?* Fresh air filled his lungs. *Is it possible war is still being waged somewhere in this world?*

Before long, his head grew heavy, and his mind wandered to a state of peacefulness not experienced in a very long time. For a moment, he dreamt of his grandparents' farm. He walked a plowed cornfield as Grandfather's tractor plodded ahead, kicking up a cloud of dust. A large rock of brown sandstone rested at the tip of a narrow furrow. When he kicked the edge of it with his boot, a small piece of dirt flew from his sole. Bending over, he scooped the rock and heaved it onto a pile of others resting under the giant oak on the hilltop. It cracked into the pile and rolled before settling onto the ground.

No death. No violence. He forgot about war and experienced the perfection of harmony in nature.

All was still.

"*Bonjour*," a soft voice whispered above him.

Frank Taylor opened his eyes. And lost his breath.

SEVEN
My Name Is Michael

A dull buzz reverberated in Michael's ears. It beckoned him from the deepest and most comfortable of slumbers. For a moment, his mind wrestled as to whether it should return to tranquil sleep. Begrudgingly, his consciousness slid back to the present like a silk handkerchief tugged from its warm, safe haven.

He remembered.

The plane crashed. He'd jumped to safety and landed in a tree.

His eyes blinked open, and directly above, pine boughs danced in the breeze. For an instant, he considered the possibility he still dreamt.

I cut myself down and stumbled...here.

Lying on his side, he lifted his head. It was like raising a chunk of lead. He tried to wiggle his toes, but pain flooded his lower half.

He wondered if being hit by a train had a similar effect on the human frame.

Michael surmised the time to be at least midmorning but to know exactly? Impossible. His Airman's watch had cracked, the hands frozen in place. In the night, his body had become wedged between the roots of two giant pine trees. Uncomfortable, though it provided the perfect hiding spot.

Once again, the reverberating buzz echoed, and he strained to hear beyond. No voices. No machines. Only a faint breeze stirred the leaves of the surrounding trees. Catching sight of a cicada in the boughs above, he realized the source of this mysterious sound.

He crawled from between the gnarled roots and flopped onto the flat, hard ground. A thin layer of grass provided little support for his aching back. Pinching the finger of one bloody leather glove, he pulled, stretched his fingers, then formed a fist, trying to work life into the hand. He reached to his belt where a survival kit dangled. Every pilot and crew member knew the drill. Fasten the "aids box" to their belts before a crash. Unfortunately, most of the men forgot to do it or were physically incapable. Others were just too busy trying to save the plane and fellow crew members. By sheer fortune, Michael had attached his before the German fighter plane shredded half of *Lucky Lady*'s wing with its 20mm flak guns.

Lucky Lady...some name.

On one elbow, he unclipped the box and raised the lid. An inventory of the contents began with five chocolate bars. He ripped into the first wrapper, bit off a chunk, and reached back inside. Benzedrine tablets... *At least these will keep me from falling asleep.* Matches, water purification tablets, and white medical adhesive tape. The roll of tape bounced into the palm of his hand, and he grinned at the irony. He needed to wrap his entire body in bandages. Two packs of gum and a compass had hidden under the roll of tape. But, upon closer examination, he saw its smashed crystal rendered the compass useless.

That's okay, Sarah, I remember.

He glanced north and his spirits lifted.

The final item, a small leather purse, contained folded maps and several thousand French francs. He stuffed the leather purse into an inner pocket of his flight jacket then stuck the last half of the chocolate bar into his mouth. Pain shot up his shoulders from the sudden movement, and he winced.

I need to get to safety. This thought weighed heavily upon him. Eluding the Nazis, staying warm, gathering food and water, and hoping to find safety on his own required help. His plane had crashed well behind enemy lines, and the land swarmed with enemy soldiers.

Father had preached grace under pressure when leading the football team into battle against an opponent. *This is much the same thing. If I fall down, I get up.* Attributes he'd learned in a game became key components for survival. *Keep fighting. Keep battling. Keep moving.*

Just solve one problem at a time.

Though the cover of darkness would be safer to travel, he needed reconnaissance and to determine his next course of action. A sitting target made an easier one, just like in football.

Once again, the familiar electronic buzz of a cicada broke just above his head.

Snapping the lid to his survival kit shut, Michael stood and straightened, testing his body. It hurt like hell. But at least he could move...kind of. He hobbled to a tree line and along a hedgerow. Thirty minutes later, he crossed a dirt road. The mechanical hum of a truck engine approached just behind a nearby hill, and he plunged forward into tall brown grass only 100 feet from the road. His heart pounded as the vehicle neared, almost to his position. Sucking in a gulp of air and holding it, he lowered his head to the earth and prayed.

Please, just keep going.

The unmistakable sound of a large vehicle swished by, and then...voices.

Damn! German voices!

Waiting until the sounds diminished, he risked a look to find the truck loaded with soldiers veer right on the road then disappear over another hill, a thin cloud of dust trailing behind.

The brush with the enemy, so close, reaffirmed what he already knew; he needed to get to safety.

Tilting his head, he breathed a sigh of relief, and mumbled, "I know where north is, but I don't know the landscape. I need to get a better view."

A massive oak tree stood on the brow of a distant hill. His back stiffened from exertion, but he rose and pressed onward until he leaned against the bark of its fat trunk. Scanning the lowest branch, he climbed, eyes watering from the agony and effort. Half an hour passed before he had his desired view and bearings.

He gauged a small town due east of his position. But, trying to find sanctuary with that many people around? Probably teeming with Gestapo and police. The town was out of the question. Open fields lay to the south and southwest. Scattered farmhouses rested northwest. A dog barked in their direction. His heart raced, and his breath caught. A German shepherd or Doberman of the Gestapo? But after a few more barks, he realized the animal did not carry the guttural growl of either dog. Just a farm mutt.

Regardless, if he stayed in the tree any longer, it would jeopardize any safety he currently possessed. He had to make a decision.

Down the trunk he slid. Every movement, every inch, excruciating until his boot soles jarred against the ground. He staggered across the narrow dirt road the German truck passed on minutes ago. A three-foot cobblestone wall ran parallel to it before the road bent right and disappeared in the direction of the town. Only the wall separated him from farmland, and he scrambled over and leaned against it, the stony protrusions digging into his aching back.

In one of the neighboring fields, a dog barked twice, and he froze.

He had to keep moving. Peeping over the wall for a split second, he scanned the area. *Nothing*. After lowering to a crouch, he hobbled next to the wall in the direction of the farthest, most secluded structure away from town.

Bolts of spasms stabbed at his limbs from the continuous strain. *The pain! I can't breathe!*

After another ten minutes, fifty yards separated him from his goal. He stared at it. A humble wooden farmhouse and nice-sized barn another fifty yards beyond. Squatting against the stone wall, he studied the barn. Separated from the house, it meant shelter, warmth, and perhaps food and water. A direct approach would be risky, but pain overwhelmed his senses.

He drew in a deep breath, trying to calm down. To think. He could wait no longer.

It seemed he had never moved so slowly in his life. One step, one breath at a time. But, after a dozen steps, his legs locked in agony. Suddenly, the front door to the house swung open and an old woman emerged alone, her gaunt form covered by a frayed coat and worn boots.

In his condition, there would be no escaping detection. Falling to his knees, he choked back pain and tears. Sickening vulnerability and loneliness swirled in his stomach.

She carried a bucket, perhaps feed for her animals. Peering out of the corner of her eye, she froze.

"*Please* help," Michael pleaded, his voice cracking from fear and pain. "I'm American."

Her eyes shot wide, and she glanced around then revolved to him on his knees. The bucket slipped from her fingers and crashed onto the ground, spilling corn husks.

He extended arms in her direction, palms up. "Please. I don't know much French. *Aider*." He drew in a deep breath, trying to calm down, and repeated, "Please...*help*. I'm American."

She stared, said nothing for a moment then blurted, “Yes, come.”

Though she didn’t smile, his spirit soared.

She beckoned him into the house and, in broken but understandable English said, “Yes, come. We help.”

He stood, staggered two steps forward, and collapsed to his knees again.

She shuffled near, grasped an arm, and tugged. “We take care of you.”

Stifling a groan of pain and fear, he winced as she pulled him to his feet.

Could he trust her? Had she invited him inside only to send someone to fetch the Gestapo?

Through the door, they walked arm in arm.

He had no choice, no other option.

At the kitchen table, an elderly man with a headful of white hair sipped from a beige cup. His gaze widened in amazement as he caught sight of Michael’s American flight uniform.

He rose quickly, his wrinkled hand extended to his wary guest. “*Américain?*”

Michael nodded.

The old man beamed a welcome. “Sit. Please. My name’s Albert.” He grinned at the woman. “My wife, Geneviève. We’re most pleased to meet you.” He mumbled a few words of French to his wife.

Again, because he spoke very little of their language, Michael had no idea if any phrase could be a betrayal in an effort to save themselves. But his quivering legs finally gave out, and he slumped into the wooden chair, near to exhaustion. A stinging pain shot throughout his body, reminding him he could go no farther.

Albert rubbed his stubbled chin. “Welcome, but uniform...must remove.” He turned and muttered to Geneviève. Striding into another room, she returned with an armful of clothes. She placed a sweater, patched work pants, battered field boots, and a burlap sack on the table.

Albert pushed the pile of clothes toward Michael. "Clothes belonged to our son. These much safer, much safer. Put uniform in bag," he said, pointing.

Suspicious, Michael narrowed his eyes, but he understood. His chances to survive without this couple's help was minimal. Knowing the money in his aids box should be used for anyone who provided assistance, he reached inside the pocket of his flight jacket and withdrew the leather purse. Pulling out 750 francs, he pressed them into the man's hand. Geneviève stared at the money resting in her husband's palm then shook her head.

"It's okay," Michael said. "I insist. Please...take it. *Merci*. Thank you."

Folding the bills, his host then tucked them into a hip pocket of his overalls and turned toward his wife. "We let you change now." The couple walked into their bedroom and closed the door.

Michael peeled the shirt over his head. Spikes of pain wracked his back and ran through his limbs. He paused to catch his breath. Grabbing the sweater off the table, he raised the fabric to his nose and inhaled. The scent of lilacs reminded him of home, and he smiled. Pulling the sweater over his shoulders, he welcomed its warmth on his arms and torso. And the other clothing? He couldn't remember the last time civilian clothes, especially clean ones, covered his body.

Stuffing his military uniform inside the bag, he sighed at the irony. Before leaving on missions, pilots and airmen were required to leave all personal items in a small burlap sack with a tag on it that contained their home address. After bombing missions, some men never returned. And when they did not gather their items, the military mailed the packs to their families.

Staring at the loaded sack, he weighed his options, which were few. He had no choice but to trust them. Despite his newfound hosts, who seemed friendly, he reached for a knife in the pantry and shoved it under his sleeve.

Just in case.

*****

Eggs sizzled in a pan as the farmwife chopped onions on a cutting board. Michael's mouth watered at the delicious scents as he sat at the kitchen table. He knew not to let his hunger interfere with any awareness of each situation he faced. He memorized his surroundings.

Fresh-hewn boards lined one of the walls. A wooden crucifix hung next to an old china cabinet. The cupboard leaned against the wall of fresh planks, covering most of it, and a white candle burned at the center of the table.

Albert appeared from another room and motioned for Michael. "Come. I want to show you something."

He trailed him into his bedroom adjacent to the kitchen.

"Here...in here." The man pointed to a small closet and beckoned Michael to follow. They crammed inside, and Albert, holding an oil lamp for light, knelt on the floor.

"Down here. If Gestapo comes, you crawl there. False wall behind kitchen. Plenty of room."

Curious, Michael fell to his knees, ignoring the jolt of pain in his lower back. He grabbed the lamp handle and peered under some shelves of clothes. A stack of old work boots leaned against the wall.

"Move boots."

Grabbing the boots, he pulled them aside, revealing a small door less than three feet in width and height.

"Open." Albert waved a hand. "It's okay."

Michael pushed the door open to reveal a passage. Light from the lamp cast inside. Though the alcove seemed narrow, perhaps two and a half feet, it ran the entire length of the kitchen and provided more than enough room for an adult to stand.

"It's a wall behind a wall," Albert said. "At end of passage, another door. It leads outside to barn."

Michael had studied the house before he'd been discovered. From outside the farmhouse, no one would notice the discrepancy of the missing sliver of kitchen. The narrow crevice provided the perfect place to lie and hide, or, if true danger presented itself, flee outside.

He smiled. "Thank you. *Merci*."

Grinning, Albert patted him on the shoulder. "Come. Time to eat."

Back protesting, he rose to his feet and limped into the kitchen. He eased into a chair and though trying not to, wolfed down eggs and toast, sipped watery coffee from a beige cup, and finally breathed a sigh of relief. *Perhaps my sanctuary has been found...for the time being.*

The couple sat opposite and watched him eat. His fork and knife clanked against the ceramic plate as he cut up the last of his food. Geneviève spoke a few words of French and tapped her husband's shoulder.

Albert nodded. "She says she'd like to give more food, but Germans stole most of our crops and livestock." Again, she spoke, and he translated. "She's sorry coffee is so watered."

Michael stopped chewing and wiped his mouth with a cloth napkin. Setting his fork onto the plate, he raised his chin and focused solely on the couple. He grasped for the right words to express his gratitude, but every single one seemed lacking.

Geneviève smiled, and it changed her face, reminding him of someone familiar. She moved behind him and, in a strangely intimate gesture, straightened his collar and patted him on the neck. A surge of emotion pounded in his heart as an image of his own grandmother flashed in his mind. And, in that moment, he knew.

He could trust them.

"I was cold, hungry, and alone. Now, I sit with you two and can't begin to thank you for what you've done for me, what you risk." Tears welled. "My name is Michael...Michael Taylor."

EIGHT

Tall Tale

Holding a deck of cards in one hand, Private First Class Haubert scratched his curly brown hair with the other. "What's the game, boys?"

"It's not your deal, Hobs." PFC Moore snatched the deck out of Haubert's fingers and began shuffling. "It's mine."

"Then what's the game?" Piero repeated.

Moore raised an eyebrow, a trademark reaction to any question. "Whores and fours, gentlemen. Ante up."

"How's it played?"

"Ahhh, come on, Z!" We've played that game three times already!" Haubert shook his head and moseyed to the rear of the tent.

Unblinking, Moore continued shuffling. "It's like seven-card stud. Two cards down, rest up, one at a time. Queens and fours wild. Bet every new card. Quarter ante."

Haubert grabbed a green satchel hidden under his pillow, pulled out a fistful of cigars, and tossed three onto the table. "Stogie, anyone? Smoke 'em if you got 'em."

Piero peeked at his two down cards and sighed. "Where's Riz?"

Moore chuckled. "Said something about getting some chow."

"I swear, that guy's got a tapeworm." Haubert bit the tip of his cigar and spat it at Piero, who didn't flinch. He flicked a match against the table, and it flared to life.

"Jack high bets." Moore elbowed the soldier to his left.

Piero reached into a small pile of coins and flipped one onto the tabletop. "Jack bets a penny."

"A penny? Really?" Moore laughed. "*Big* spender!"

Haubert's pressed lips bounced a cigar with each syllable he muttered. "You know what the best sound in the world is?"

Moore interrupted, "Pair a twos bets."

"The sound of a ball hitting the sweet spot?" Piero's hand started for a cigar but drew back to his cards.

"Pair bets. It's to you...*Piero*!" Moore swatted his cheek. "Damn bugs."

Haubert flashed a grin. "Bucks bustin' through the woods and smallmouth jumpin' on your fishin' line."

"I fold," Piero said.

"We just started!" Moore shook his head. "How can you fold already? You know, Z, if you brought more than *two* dollars to the table every time we played, you'd last a little longer."

"That's all right. I'll watch you guys..." Piero frowned. "Think Sarge is okay?"

Haubert stared at the cards in his grip. "Better be. He got two days to get his ass back."

Without warning, the entrance flap to the tent tore open and PFC Risaliti crashed inside. A blanket wrapped around a small object was cradled in his arms.

The men froze. Riz darted to the corner, laid the object down, and returned to the entrance. Sticking his head back outside, he scanned the perimeter.

"What're you *doing*?" Moore's left eyebrow arched high into his forehead.

"Making sure I wasn't followed." Risaliti whipped his head back inside and snapped the flap shut. "Good. Coast is clear." Dashing to the corner, he retrieved the wrapped bundle. "Make way."

"Is it a boy or a girl?" Piero joked.

Riz plopped the blanket onto the table. "Gentlemen, I present..." Grabbing a corner of the olive-green blanket, he ripped it away, revealing a large tin can. "The finest beef stew, courtesy of the US Army."

Haubert's jaw dropped. The stogie tumbled from his lips and plopped in his lap. Ash sprayed everywhere. "You gotta be kiddin' me!"

"I never kid when it comes to food. I found it just lying there...in the supply tent." Risaliti pulled a can opener from his pocket and tossed it onto the table. "Piero, open this."

"Yes, sir." Piero saluted, plunged the opener into the lid, and cranked. The men abandoned the card game and scampered to find their mess kits.

Risaliti retreated to the corner of the tent and pulled three loaves of French bread from under a blanket.

"*Where'd* you get those?" Moore's husky voice barked.

"*Shhh*, not so loud. I traded some chocolate bars at that small farmhouse on the west side of camp.

"Well, I'll give you credit. You're a man who knows how to get things." Moore stubbed his cigarette out on the sole of his boot and saved the rest for later in his shirt pocket. "I could use a man like you when this war's over."

"Gentlemen!" Risaliti's voice was more aristocrat than soldier. "*Bon appétit!*"

"I don't know about you boys, but I'm gonna eat like I'm going to the ch-ch-chair." Piero's fork plunged into the can. "Good job, Riz!"

Haubert unsheathed his knife and hacked a thick slice of baguette.

The "poker" table quickly morphed into an "evening snack" table. The men ate voraciously, in military fashion.

"You know..." Risaliti stabbed another forkful of stew. "The shit you take care of as a soldier, you don't see anywhere else."

"Ain't that the truth." Haubert turned to Moore. The private nodded with a mischievous grin. The battle plan was set in motion. "You guys ever hear 'bout what happened to Major General Hoover?" A piece of meat shot from Haubert's lips, but he ignored it.

Piero shook his head.

Moore played along with his buddy's banter. "He's the major general from Texas, isn't he? The one that can't hear so well?"

"Yep, hard of hearin' in his left ear. Can't hear a *durn* thing." Haubert traded the fork in his mouth for a fresh cigar. "Goes back to a farmin' accident he had in the states before the war. Apparently, when he's just a kid, he's mendin' a fence when one of his cows snuck up on him. He turned 'round and there behind him...a Texas Longhorn. Ever seen one, Z?"

"Never."

"Well, imagine a steer 'bout four-and-a-half feet high with horns on his head like wings on a C-47. Now, usually, they're rather gentle creatures and known to be smart...for cattle, that is. The story goes that even though Hoover were just a *wee* little boy of ten years old, he decides he's gonna try and ride that Longhorn cuz he heard it couldn't be done. Weighed darn near two thousand pounds, it did!"

Piero's voice raised an octave in amazement. "Two *thousand*?"

"Two thousand pounds of prime Texas beef." Haubert fished a strand of beef out of his tooth with a fingernail. "Now, a Longhorn, like I already mentioned, can stand four-and-a-half feet high, so Major General Derrick Hoover decides to get *waaay* behind 'em and jump on. But he needs to get a runnin' start. He sidles behind that cow and starts at the hindside in a dead sprint. *Just* as he jumps, that longhorn kicks back with all his might, catchin' the major general square in the ear with his hoof."

Piero's eyes shot wide. He glanced at the men around the table, mouth agape.

"Rumor has it that poor boy was kicked so hard, he flew backward through the fence he was mendin'. After flyin' through the fence, he busted a small oak tree and kept right on going. Smack into the side of a *big* hill. Knocked out cold, he was." PFC Haubert drummed his tobacco-stained fingers on the tabletop. "Now here's where the story gets good."

Risaliti shoveled another forkful of stew and shook his head.

"He hit that hillside *so* hard, oil started ta spurt out. When he woke, he found himself surrounded by a pool of black gold. Family made millions when they realized what that farm sat on. Biggest oil deposit west of the Mississippi...and that's why they named 'em derricks."

"Who?" Piero leaned forward in his chair and rubbed his pug-like nose. "Named what derricks?"

"Those *big* towers that drill for oil. That's why they're called derricks, because of *our* Major General Derrick Hoover! Hit the ground so hard in the summer of '04, oil came squirtn' out."

Moore arched a brow and turned to Piero. "That's why if you ever talk to the major general, *never* speak into his left ear. *Never*. He finds it insulting. If you do find yourself standing on that side...well, you better just yell 'bout as loud as you can because his hearing ain't so good in his right one, either."

"And if there's one thing that irritates the old man?" Risaliti jammed his fork into a piece of meat. "It's a low talker."

"A low talker?" Piero asked.

"Ya know, someone who whispers all the time, talks too damn quiet," Haubert said. "A low talker."

"Wow! I had no idea. Thanks for letting me know." Piero cupped both hands behind his head and leaned back in his chair. His face lit with a glimmer of satisfaction, like a child finally solving a riddle. "So, that's why they're called derricks. I'll be damned."

NINE
Song of Cigale

Frank Taylor opened his eyes. And lost his breath.

She strode into view, shining in her youth and beauty. She had wonderfully dark hair, and he watched her brush a wind-blown strand from her face with the back of her delicate hand. In a single moment, something changed inside of Frank. The concept of time ceased to exist. Only the pounding of his heart reminded him he just sat there, watching her.

Everything about her exuded grace. The way she moved, every gesture, even the way she stood as the breeze caressed her blue dress across her slender form.

He peered into her deep-violet eyes. Warmth and softness shone through. Every thought and feeling of hers revealed itself with the simplest of looks. But there was more. The same vulnerability a flower has that awaits morning frost, her bearing had. Perhaps it was a hint of something that had wounded her long ago.

"*Bonjour*." The word echoed as if spoken from the summit of *Le Bec D'Aigle*.

He found his breath. "*Bonjour*."

"You're American?"

"Yes."

"*Why* are you here?"

Her tone stuck Frank as rather fierce, and he admired it. "I'm waiting for my friend. I brought him home to see his family. I'm..."

Arthur's voice rang in the distance. "*Caroline*?"

In an instant, she spun. "Arthur?"

He fell into a sprint.

"*Arthur?*" she cried, rushing to meet him.

"Caro!"

They sprang into each other's arms. Frank stood in the wake of their happiness and streams of tears.

"Oh, Arthur!"

"Caro..." Arthur searched his sister's countenance with a desperate look. "*Papa et Maman*. Where?"

Her gaze fell to the ground. "Arthur, my dear brother..." Her voice dissolved into quick gasps. Then, as if not wanting their reunion to end, she finally broke the embrace, linked her arm in his and led him into the house. "Come inside. I have much to tell you."

*****

Caro leaned forward and struck a match across the wooden tabletop. Her hand paused before lifting the match to the white candle sitting at the table's center. The wick flared to life, illuminating her face in flickering light, and Frank could not keep from staring. She exhaled deeply and sat a moment in silence.

"That night, I ran. I hid in the boathouse, waiting as *Père et Mère* instructed. I heard cars and German shouts. I prayed they'd leave." Caro grasped the silver locket around her neck and pinched it between her thumb and index finger. Her voice barely above a whisper, she said, "I lay there, in the loft, frozen with fear. That's when I heard four...sounds."

Arthur sat at the kitchen table next to her, his expression unflinching, like the hunchback of stone just beyond the bay. Reaching for her shoulder, he patted with a reassuring touch. "It's okay, Caro. Go on."

Frank stood in the dark corner of the kitchen, not daring to move, his nerves on edge as he anticipated her answer.

"I didn't see, but heard...four pops in the night, and it was over. I *knew*. I knew in my heart. They died to protect me. That night, lying in the loft, exhausted, I sang myself to sleep." A thin, tired smile spread on her lips. "The same song *Maman* sang to us, when we were children afraid of a storm."

"At first light the next morning, I descended." The anguish in her voice shifted to incredulity. "They left them, Arthur. The Germans...just left them *lying* there." She reached for a glass of wine and gulped. "Somehow, *Papa*...crawled...to *Maman*. That's how they died. In each other's arms and I could do...noth—" The glassware clinked on the tabletop, and she buried her head in hands, sobbing.

Arthur's eyes filled with tears. They rolled and fell, absorbed quickly by the tabletop. But his voice remained firm. "They died protecting *us*. They died protecting *France*. *Please*, don't blame yourself, Caro. The Germans will pay." He leaned forward and drew her close. "They will pay," he repeated quietly.

Frank stood frozen at the edge of the candlelight. His mind raced to thoughts of his own parents. But they were in the States. Safe.

"*Où*? Where?" Arthur asked. "Where are Mother and Father...buried?" Frank heard the crack in his voice.

"That morning, with Uncle Jean's help, I took them to the cemetery." Caro pulled back and sighed. "They rest next to Grandmother and Grandfather, beneath the twisted poplars."

"You are so strong, Caro. Never doubt that. So very strong. I'm proud of you." His expression turned thoughtful, as if he drew strength from his sister's touch. "Always remember, they did not die in vain. Their information saved thousands and soon will liberate France."

"Arthur? Where do we go from here? What do we—?"

"*You* must endure. We must *all* endure." A gritty resolve gripped his next words. "Evil will reap what it has sowed."

Her look, bloodshot and raw, caught Frank's.

His heart cleaved, as if a spike drove through it. Yet, her violet eyes held him, and the pain coursing through her body flowed into his. He stepped forward, out of darkness of shadow, focused solely on the beautiful innocence of this woman, who, moments ago, had robbed his breath. "Your brother's right, Caroline. We're here so you'll never live in fear." Frank stood tall, his jaw set in firm determination. "All you hold dear will bloom again, in peace. I promise."

Outside, a three-foot stone wall bordered both sides for the first ten minutes of the walk then the road became narrower and hilly. The wall sloped downward before disappearing into the distance. The country road leading to the cemetery wound through orchards and rolling fields. Groves of pine trees wavered in the soft, warm breeze just beyond the walls, and cast lacy shadows before their feet.

"Through here." Arthur reached for a rusted iron gate and swung it open.

Caro strode to the front of the three-person procession. Light steps carried her onto a gravel path that snaked through marble markers and weathered tombstones and to the back edge of the cemetery.

She paused before two giant poplars that stood protectively over the plots. Their lean, blanched trunks coiled around the other as if frozen for eternity in a lover's embrace. "Here. This is where...they're buried."

Arthur took three small steps forward and sank to his knees. Shoulders slumped, he combed fingers through the thin, young grass of the fresh plot. Filling his lungs with breath, he clutched a handful of green and exhaled.

Then a faint smile crossed his lips. "Father worked in the shipyard when he was seventeen. After earning enough money, he bought a boat and started to fish. He named the boat *Petite Fleur* because he called

Mother his 'little flower.'" He spoke with an exaggerated earnestness, as if fighting back his emotion. "When I was six, he taught me how to fish. The night before our first expedition I was so excited, I couldn't sleep. I struggled under the weight of the mast that morning but swelled with pride because Father treated me like a man. Then, sitting by my side, he patiently showed me how to tie a proper knot and keep a line straight. I still remember the taste of the air and when the line came to life with the fighting of the fish."

Frank glanced at Caro then turned his attention back to Arthur.

"Mother rented a sewing machine before marrying. It wasn't long before everyone in town brought her clothes to mend...the seamstress of *La Ciotat*. The extra money provided us with piano lessons at church." He threw his head back and stared at a sky so blue, it verged into purple. "It's so beautiful today. So...peaceful." His lower lip quivered, and he blinked back tears. "I'm sorry. I'm so sorry, Caro, for not...being here. I could have..."

Caro knelt beside her brother. Extending an arm around his heaving shoulders, she gently pulled his head onto her shoulder. "Shhh...*mon cher frère...mon frère chéri*." Her raven hair dazzled in sunlight and danced with the breeze.

Suddenly, Frank was an intruder. Gravel shifted beneath feet as he pivoted on the path, marched through the gateway, and returned to Arthur's home. Walking to the flower bed at the front of the house, he bent down on one knee and caught a scent of fresh earth. One by one, he grabbed weeds and pulled. *This feels good.* Soon, a single rose bush revealed itself and then another. *This feels right.* He took quiet satisfaction in the familiar labor. Lately, the only time he fell and touched the ground was to dig a foxhole.

Flecks of black dirt dotted his forearms and wrists. *Dirt...* He chuckled to himself. *At least dirty hands clean easier than bloody ones.*

Frank swiped his sweat-soaked face with his sleeve and stood up. Pulling a knife from the sheath on his belt, he maneuvered around each bush until he held a bouquet of roses. Footsteps echoed behind, and he peered over a shoulder to see Arthur and Caro watching. Frank wiped the blade clean on the back of his pant leg. "I'm guessing this isn't a typical sight?"

They stared at him with happy amazement. "You've been busy, my friend," Arthur said.

Frank extended the flowers to Caro. "These are for you."

Her face brightened and she cradled the bouquet as if grasping a newborn. "*Merci.*"

"All you hold dear will bloom again. I promise." Frank sheathed the knife at his side.

"Do you always keep true to your promises, Frank Taylor?" Caro plucked a snow-white bloom from the bouquet and tucked the blossom behind one ear. The ivory rose petals contrasted sharply with her dark hair.

Frank drank in a long look of her.

"I left a change of clothes for you in my room. Get cleaned, relax. Tomorrow, I must check with neighbors and friends, but tonight we enjoy the beauty of La Ciotat." Arthur led the way into the house, and Frank peeked back over his shoulder.

The wind played with Caro's hair. Still cradling her flowers, she glanced into his eyes and down to the bouquet she held. And for the first time since he'd met her, she smiled. It lived in every part of her face. He even noticed a dimple on her cheek that, until now, had gone unseen.

Then, Frank Taylor did something he never imagined possible in war. He opened his heart and surrendered.

*****

The next afternoon, Arthur stood at the counter, opening another bottle of wine. Sunlight poured through a window and lit the upper half of his body like a spotlight on stage. Freshly showered, he'd shed his military uniform for pressed black slacks and a white button-down. Caro washed dishes in the sink and passed them to Frank, who dried. He leaned toward her to make it easier for her to give him the plates but mostly just to be closer.

He breathed in a hint of her perfume. "*Merci.* Thank you for supper. I haven't had a home-cooked meal in...to be honest, I can't remember. It was excellent."

"My pleasure."

"What was it like here, when you were children?" Frank placed a dry dish onto a stack of others.

"Before the war, we played like any sister and brother," Caro said.

"And fought..." A cork popped softly as Arthur pulled it from the wine bottle. "Like any brother and sister."

"Arthur helped Father fish, and I worked in the bakery with Aunt and Uncle. Summer afternoons, we'd walk the hills beyond town and look for *des cigales.*" She passed Frank another dish.

Frank shrugged. "*Cigales?*"

Arthur's thumb and finger indicated a small object. "Cicadas. Little insects that fly and make music with their wings."

Frank nodded in understanding.

"We'd make a house for them in small cardboard boxes and search the countryside, drawn by their hypnotic song. When we found them, we took them home," Caro said. Frank's fingertips brushed hers while he reached for the next plate. Her attention darted to the sink, a glimmer of blush on her cheeks.

"And my dear sister would *always* sing to them," Arthur added.

"I wanted to hear *them* sing. I would find fresh leaves and feed them flowers. But *des cigales*, cicadas...they never sang. They never ate. And soon died, always. After a while, we felt bad and stopped catching them and taking them home."

"They could not be held captive," Arthur said.

"They are like us." She said confidently. "They never sang in captivity, and if I were them, I, too, would die before singing."

"Well, Sister, you are not in captivity. Nor will you be." Arthur offered Frank a glass of red wine. "It seems to me we've not had song nor laughter for so very long. Too long. *Caro*?"

Shutting the water off at the sink, she turned and stared at her brother.

"Could you sing for us now? I have not heard you for—" he began.

"Arthur, I don't know if—"

"Honor our guest with one song. I know you are not shy in sharing your magical voice."

She shook her head. "Arthur, I—"

"My sister's called *l'ange de La Ciotat* because everyone knows her voice is the sound of angels' wings."

Relenting, she asked, "Frank, would you hear a *chanson*?"

"I'm not sure what a *chanson* is, but if that's a song, yes. I'd be honored. *Oui.*"

"Frank! Your French..." Arthur chuckled. "It's improving!"

Their laughter filled the house. Caro stood next to the kitchen table and straightened her back. "I have not heard laughter in this house for so very long." She tilted her head and combed fingers through her short raven hair, revealing her strikingly beautiful and youthful face, her skin flawless. "I will sing for you, Frank Taylor."

Frank sipped his wine and sat next to Arthur. Warmth from the cabernet surged throughout his head and fingertips. The candle's flame next to his elbow added a magical aura and radiance to her shimmering figure. Caro's presence held him spellbound.

She twisted the silver locket between her fingers.

Then silence gave way to innocent voice, startling him, the sound incredibly large and filling the room with an angelic presence.

Au clair de la lune,
Mon ami Pierrot,
Prête-moi ta plume
Pour écrire un mot.

Transfixed, Frank slumped in his chair and shut his eyes. Even without sight, the absolute beauty of her voice filled his soul with peacefulness the war could never offer. And as he listened, there were no more thoughts about death and hurt and violence.

Au clair de la lune,
Pierrot répondit:
Je n'ai pas de plume,
Je suis dans mon lit.

Emotion, buried under years of combat, flowed over him. Through him. *I have forgotten.* He had forgotten what human felt like.

Au clair de la lune,
On n'y voit qu'un peu
On chercha la plume,
On chercha du feu.

Breathless once again, he opened his eyes.

Arthur leaned to his sister and kissed her lightly on the cheek. "*Magnifique.* Simply *magnifique.* And still wearing my gift, I see." He fingered the locket.

"I will never remove it," she said, looking down.

"And I will never tire of your singing. Your sweet voice reminds me of old times...of happy times."

Her smile filled her face with joy. "Like grand-mère's bedtime stories?"

"Oui."

Tucking a strand of hair behind her ear with the back of a finger, she met Frank's stare. "Every night at bedtime, when we were children, she would tell us a magical story of La Ciotat's birth."

"Would you share the story? With me? Now?" he asked.

She nodded in agreement. "The titanic rock's violent upward angle suggested a primordial battle had once been waged. Perched on the absolute edge of the coastline of southern France, the monolith thrust itself over five-hundred feet skyward, and the sheer size of it was comparable to that of a small island."

"Perhaps, in the beginning..."—Arthur's words echoed between the wood walls of the kitchen..."—the land had become angry at the water's infringement, and, in a show of power, heaved a small part of itself as a declaration against further intrusion. Or perhaps the sea tried to demonstrate its dominance by attempting to swallow land, but, upon failure to ingest this massive formation, admitted defeat. These myths of violent origin could not be further from the truth."

Caro's skin glittered with candlelight, and she continued, "This was a marriage of land and sea. And the menacing facade of stone was not the result of some heated dispute that questioned which was mightier, land or water. Rather, it affirmed itself as nothing more than a loving consequence of earth's embrace, and the combination of land and water created a hidden jewel beneath the heavens. Centuries passed, and the giant hunchback of rock existed in absolute harmony with the Mediterranean." She nodded ever so slightly to Arthur.

"Tucked behind the protective shadow of a sentinel of stone, a tiny coastal village of fishermen, bakers, and churchgoing people went about their daily lives. Their humble homes lined the shore, and fishing boats filled the bay with enough color that any rainbow dissolved into jealousy. Deepest blues of sky matched those of sea, and left all in between framed with a clarity of light unfamiliar to outsiders."

She walked to the window and unlatched it. A single ray of sunlight filtered through the opening, and she turned back to the table. "Inhabitants knew quite well they were sheltered from the northwest mistral by their giant sentinel of rock. For when the wind did blow, it whispered an intoxicating spell of good health and patience. Its incantation measured time not by day or night but rather in the purest of ways."

Arthur raised his wineglass. "The variety of wine sitting on the table, type of clothing worn by children playing in the streets, or fragrance of which flower bloomed, and which did not, provided the subtlest clues necessary for life and time. And every evening, before the setting sun fell, golden light splashed terracotta roofs, sides of buildings illuminated, boats and waters shimmered, and children's faces glowed."

"For in this small corner of the universe..."— Caro's words rang faraway and dreamlike— "all seemed right in La Ciotat."

Frank stared at them, still absorbing the tale. "My God, that was beautiful. All I got every night on the farm was a chance to milk the cows a second time."

Laughter erupted in the quaint room.

Four quick raps sounded on the door, and everyone froze. In one fluid motion, Arthur spun and pulled a handgun tucked in the back of his pants. He gestured for Caroline to do the speaking while he tiptoed beside the entrance. Frank snatched his rifle leaning against the corner of the kitchen wall. Raising it, he aimed at the center of the door.

"*Qui est là*?" Caro asked politely.

A husky voice replied, "Claude."

Arthur cracked the door and peered outside then back to Frank with a reassuring nod. "It's okay. A friend." He opened the door, and a rail-thin man dressed in denim overalls that had seen better days limped through the doorway. Smoky shadows circled his eyes. Removing his black beret, he tucked it under his armpit.

Frank lowered his rifle and leaned it in the corner. Arthur embraced the man, and they spoke in whispers of French.

Caro went to Frank. "They were boyhood friends. Claude checks in every so often, like a big brother. He's Maquis. He and others like him do what they can to slow the flow of goods from France to Germany."

"He's a soldier," Frank said flatly.

"He *was* a farmer, like his father. Like all Maquis, Claude lives in the shadows. They bomb trains, blow up munition dumps, and disrupt German shipping in the harbor. And though it may not appear, he has the heart of a lion. He and Arthur are the same age. Boyhood friends."

"Life in the shadows has taken a toll. It is sad."

She lifted one eyebrow. "It is war."

"Change of plans. There's a meeting tonight." Floorboards creaked as Arthur stepped toward Frank. "A weapons drop is scheduled in three days, and I've been asked to help make preparations."

"Do you need help? I'd be happy to..."

"No. You've done more than enough. You brought me home. Trust me on this. You stay here, my friend. Relax. Besides, I must also go into town and check with others. All of this easier tonight, moving in the dark. I won't return until morning. I need you to look after Caroline while I'm gone."

"You're sure?" Frank asked.

"*Oui*. When I return, we leave for Le Muy."

"Of course." Frank nodded. "Be safe."

Arthur kissed each of Caro's cheeks. "You understand? I must go?"

"It is war," she said, her voice almost inaudible.

"It is. I will see you soon, Sister." He grabbed a small black backpack and half a baguette from the counter then strode toward Claude. "*Au revoir,*" he muttered over his shoulder.

The door closed behind them.

*****

Sitting next to Frank at the kitchen table, she caressed the rim of her wineglass with the tip of a finger. Her eyes met his.

"Your singing was...I think even the angels would be jealous."

Caro's faint smile seemed weighted with sadness.

Neither spoke for a while, creating an awkward silence.

Finally, Frank blurted, "Arthur told me your father liked wine, especially in his soup?"

"He did." Her face lit with memory. "Rosé in the summer. Merlot in winter. Did he tell you any other family secrets?"

"No." He sipped his wine. "Nothing incriminating."

"Father would loosen his belt during meals. Mother would kid him for making too much room to eat." Caro leaned back into the creaking wooden chair and crossed her legs. "Tell me where you're from, Frank."

"A state called Kansas. It's smack dab in the middle of the United States. A small town—Thompsonville. A large portion of my childhood was spent on my grandparents' farm. My brother and I would help them with plowing, planting, and milking." He reached for a small piece of wheat bread plated on the table and nibbled. "This bread is excellent."

"Years ago, my great-grandfather started a bakery in town."

"The one your aunt and uncle run? The one you and Arthur stopped at after school?"

"*Oui*. How did you—?"

"Arthur told me when we first arrived."

"My aunt and uncle, over the course of time, took the shop over. My uncle's a very kind man, but one morning when I was very young, he yelled at me for sneaking cookies, and I cried. I forgave him that same day because everything tasted so good." Caroline swirled the wine in her glass. "He's been kind to me ever since."

"When I'm in trouble, when things don't look good when we're in combat, I try to stay calm by remembering things that make me smile." Frank downed the remaining wine in his glass. "Perhaps I'll remember this."

"Aunt Margaret, Uncle Jean's wife, always makes me laugh. And though my uncle likes to think he's in charge, *she* runs the bakery. She always wears a large, starched apron and keeps it immaculate. When a child, I called it her shield of protection. Every morning as the first batch of warm bread came out of the oven, I'd be at her side. Aunt called me her *petite main* or little hand." Caro giggled at the sweet reminiscence and stared into the candlelight with a dreamy expression. "I always had my choice of first loaf. You know,

Frank"—her fingertip trailed the rim of the glass—"it is good to laugh in times like these. Until you came, I had almost forgotten how."

"Yes. Yes, it is." He set his wineglass on the table and stood. "I'm going to clean up and change. Then, would you walk with me to the ocean?"

"Of course." She raised her glass and took another sip.

Frank smiled, walked into a bedroom, and closed the door behind him. He rolled his sleeves and dipped both hands into a basin set on a dresser. The cool water trickled between his fingers. Bending down, he splashed his face. *I'm a battle-hardened sergeant, and this nineteen-year-old French girl is tugging my heartstrings as if she owns them.* He shook his head to clear the excess water and his thoughts. A woman could do strange things to a man's soul.

*****

"My brother's clothes look good on you, but here..." Caro straightened the collar of the white shirt. "Now, you look proper."

"*Merci.*"

Exiting the house, they strolled along the path leading to the boathouse and descended the hill toward the Mediterranean. Despite the late hour, the day had grown warmer, and the sun beat down on their heads. The sunlight was broken by random shadows of palm and poplar trees.

"Southern France has many poplar trees," Frank said.

"Every July, the people of La Ciotat plant them as a symbol of strength."

"So, that's why they're everywhere."

"We had a special tree called *l'arbre de la liberté* or the tree of liberty. It was part of a special ceremony, and for some years I was chosen to sing at it. But war came to our world and tradition came to an end."

"Caro..." He jerked to a halt. "*Listen.*" The trill of a cicada crescendoed near them. "There! On the tree."

Her voice rose in excitement. "I haven't heard one for so very long." A familiar clicking screech reverberated into a heightened pitch then abruptly faded into a diminishing electronic buzz.

He pointed to a bough just out of reach.

"I think their sound is the song of summer," she said. "But it is strange."

"What is?"

"I don't find them this close to the sea. It must be lost."

"Or perhaps..." He turned to Caro. Her violet eyes met his, and he found himself at barely a breath's distance from her lips. "Perhaps he just wanted to find you."

Her cheeks flushed with excitement.

Frank inhaled the scent of her lavender perfume, and his skin prickled. *How can this happen so fast?* For a moment, he wanted only one thing...to kiss this woman who had stolen his breath—and now, his heart.

"We're almost there." She took the lead, reached back, and pulled him by the hand.

They wound around the final bend, and the white boathouse stood before them. The vastness of sea stretched next to it, and, to its right across the bay, the hunchback of three great rocks lined the horizon, silhouetted by the setting sun behind.

"This place is amazing. Are those the hills of stone from your bedtime story?"

"*Oui.*" Her raven hair bounced off tanned shoulders. "There is something so simply wonderful about a sunset. Don't you think?"

He chuckled to himself as she pressed forward. *And something divinely wonderful when you can share it with someone you're in love with.*

Streaks of aurous light glimmered across the water's surface, and he shielded his eyes from the glare. He stepped onto the soft shore. Placid waves lapped against whitish sand, and the tranquil sound created a hypnotic feeling deep within. "I know this feeling." He turned to Caro.

The wind played carelessly with her hair, distracting him for a moment.

"It was an afternoon thunderstorm on my grandfather's farm, and I just stood in the rain, not caring. My hair dripping wet. My clothes soaked. I was chilled to the bone. And as the dark clouds rolled past, golden light filtered through the remaining mist and onto the leaves of the tallest trees and onto me, standing there in the open field. *Everything* was golden. *Everything* seemed right with the world."

She leaned into his arm and pointed at the sea. "It's as if both water and air are fashioned of gold."

"That's the last time I felt this...peaceful, this relaxed." Bordering the shore nearby stood a small bleached wooden structure, weathered by years of salt and sun. Its worn whiteness contrasted sharply with the deep-blue water. "Your father's boathouse?"

"Follow me. I want to show you something." Caro opened the door and stepped inside. "Come." She waved for him to follow. Once inside, she moved to a wooden ladder.

"Where're you going?"

In a matter of seconds, she jumped into the loft and peered down. "Frank Taylor, don't you jump from airplanes? You cannot be afraid of heights."

"I want you to know"—he threw a hand on a rung and gripped it—"I grew up in a barn, and height is not a problem." Frank climbed the ladder as Caro moved to the far corner.

Caro reached above, pulled at a tile of terracotta roof, and set it to the side. A slanted ray of light streamed through.

"Over here." Caro knelt below the opening. "Soon, the light of *la première étoile*, the first star, will light the night sky. When we were young, Arthur and I played in this loft and watched for stars. He gave me this for my birthday." She reached for the chain under her blue dress. Delicate silver links glittered beneath her fingers. With her thumb and forefinger, she flicked open the locket to reveal a family picture. "This was taken on my birthday."

Frank peered at the image. "Your aunt and uncle?"

"*Oui*," she whispered softly.

"And that's Arthur?" Frank beamed.

"And my mother and father."

"Happy times."

"The best of times." Suddenly, Caro's expression drooped with sadness.

In an effort to reassure, Frank slid a hand to hers. "The best of times will return, Caro, I promise. War brings out the worst in humanity. But I believe it can also reveal what is best in life."

"Such as?" she asked, violet eyes wide.

"Well, there is the ocean and the sun." Frank paused. "Flowers and mountains and the sky."

Caro nodded, inviting him to continue.

"And sunrises and sunsets. There is kindness, truth, and hope." He swallowed hard, unable to look away from her. "There is laughter...and cicadas."

Caro giggled.

"And beauty." For a moment, Frank lost himself. A warm flush and sense of boldness filtered through his body from the wine drunk earlier. "And most of all, there is love, Caro. There is *always* love." Both stared at each other, their soft breath the only sound.

"And what do you know of love?"

"I know it's pure and honest. I know that when it finds you, it wraps itself around your heart with an iron grip and won't let go. And it's the only thing that makes this damn war worth fighting." Any trace of nervousness between them vanished.

Caro tilted her head and searched the twilight sky through the aperture. Her hair fell carelessly around her shoulders. Pale light shimmered off each strand like misty drops hovering above a moonlit waterfall. Frank breathed in, and in a little more than a whisper, spoke. "Times like these teach us not to take anything for granted, for what is here today may be gone tomorrow. Sometimes, it forces us to live faster than we'd like, to make the most of the time we have."

"You've a way with words, Frank Taylor." Caro paused, and her voice trailed into a whisper. "I need to tell you something. I *want* to tell you."

He shrugged. "What?"

"With all my heart, *merci*."

Frank's eyes narrowed.

She grabbed a single piece of straw from the loft's bed. "For bringing my brother home. It means more to me than you could ever know."

"It was nothing."

Their gazes met, held. "It is *everything*." She rolled the straw between her fingers. "Now, what would you like to do?"

He snared a piece and plucked at it. "I like open spaces, no walls. After the war, I've thought of finding some land. I've always wanted to own my own mountain. Maybe have some horses, perhaps my own ranch." The straw bounced between his rolling fingers. "But that seems like another life from this one. And I still have this crazy war to think about. The thing about the future is we spend so much time looking for it, but we never see it coming."

"I *mean*..." Caro asked with the playfulness of a child, yet the words emerged from the inviting lips of an unquestionable woman. "What would you like to do *now*?"

Despite the dim light, her youthful skin illuminated with an intoxicating glow. Everything "war" was forgotten, of another lifetime.

Frank no longer held back. "I want to kiss you. I've *always* wanted to kiss you."

Leaning in, the warmth of her cheeks and neck radiated through his fingers. Ever so delicate, their mouths met.

This was not the imaginary moment he'd longed for. It was real, and he savored every second.

Frank pulled slowly away and let his fingers slip through her dark hair like a comb. His fingertips dropped to her shoulders, her silky skin warmly inviting. Then, he extended a single finger, tracing the length of her tanned arm before returning to her ebony hair.

Caro's skin shook in excitement. She nuzzled his neck, and he caught a hint of perfume. It was like breathing fire.

Every pore burned in passion.

Both their bodies sank into the straw bed. Soft kisses met with soft kisses, and then their tongues met.

Passion exploded. Tender kisses turned from delicacy and excitement to something else. Mouths became hungry and searching. Licking the lobe of her ear, he breathed into it. "From the moment I saw you..." He raised his leg over hers and rolled next to her. "I knew."

Caro's fingers fumbled with buttons on Frank's shirt then his pants. He helped her dress slide off. Each gripped the other, and a rising heat consumed every thought but one. Caro bit his lower lip playfully, kissed his neck, and pulled him on top. Neither held back.

She clung to him with legs and arms and pulled him in. His chest to her breasts, his naval to hers, his face buried in her hair.

Warmth surged throughout their bodies. Their eyes found each other. Pleasure and elation rolled into one giant wave.

The feeling swelled and rose until, finally, both shuddered and collapsed. Sweat-soaked bodies intertwined, exhausted.

For an instant, they caught each other's glance and smiled.

He slung his arm over her chest. With each of her panting breaths, his arm moved in unison with her body. Caro quivered one final time. The madness dissipated.

Finally, their breathing slowed and became one.

A cone of moonlight poured through the opening, causing part of her form to glow a diffused pale. With his lightest touch, Frank raised a hand, extended a single finger, and traced her profile. It was a profile that could break any man's heart. *So beautiful...*

She whispered, eyes closed, "What did you know?"

His fingertip slid down the slope of her petite nose, outlined gentle lips, fell to her chin, and started over.

"What did you know?" she repeated. "When you saw me?"

Leaning his lips to hers, he hovered just out of reach. The warmth of her exhale blanketed his cheeks. "Of all I know in this world, *you* are what is best and good and right."

Her mouth rounded into a smile. "*Je m'endors sur ces douces paroles.*"

"I don't...understand."

"I sleep on these sweet words."

Lying by her side, he watched her breathe.

How precious! How wonderful!

Frank did not know the time, but the depth of his own weariness was certain. Not wanting the moment to end, he again raised a single finger. But, this time, his fingertip slipped below her chin, onto her chest, and brushed the metallic links of her chain.

Knowing she slept soundly, he whispered into her ear, “So graceful, intelligent...I have known from the moment I first saw you.” He rested his head on her chest. Caro’s heart beat strong and true. “If only I could escape my life for *this*—for *you*.” His eyelids, heavy with sleep, could no longer fight bone-deep weariness.

Frank dreamt of war and the lone oak atop Grandfather’s farm and cicadas.

*****

Early the next morning, Frank’s eyes flickered open, his head still lying on Caro’s chest. He listened to the steady beat of her heart. Her small fingers twirled the curls of his hair with tenderness. Rising up on one elbow, he looked upon her face. Light trickled through the aperture above them.

“This isn’t a dream?” he asked.

“This isn’t a dream,” she repeated.

Her French accent always gave him chills. “Last night, I did dream. I dreamt I was back on my grandfather’s farm in one of his fields. A large hill lies at the center, and on top is a huge oak tree...must be over a hundred years old. It’s the only tree standing there. I call it One Tree Hill. Grandpa never had the heart to cut it down when the tree was much smaller and he quite younger.” Frank’s head fell again to her chest. “The tree is surrounded by rocks pulled from the field so they wouldn’t dull the plows.”

Caro’s fingers twirled one lock of his hair then the next.

"In winter months, the tree looks frozen in time. The rocks just lying at its base. It always looked so frigid and so alone up there. Everything covered with snow. The wind blows relentlessly on that hilltop." Frank drew a deep breath. "And every year, after spring planting, seeds sprout to life, and the giant tree looks like...like a gentle shepherd gathering its flock...a lone sentinel on guard." Frank's fingers moved to the silver locket laying on her soft, tanned skin. "Life is funny, Caro. It goes on. It always finds a way." But the tone of Frank's voice plunged like a cold rock tossed into dark water. "I must leave today with your brother."

"Where will you go?"

"We must rejoin our unit and head north. This is the final push."

"The breath before the storm."

Frank sat up. With the faintest of touch, his lips met hers. "You're my breath now."

Caro's fingernails caressed the back of his neck, and sparks of excitement flew along his spine.

"And though I don't want to, we must go. Before your brother returns."

They dressed and emerged from the boathouse splashed in morning light. In the distance, golden rays walked upon the small town of La Ciotat.

Frank's lips pressed into a smile. "Caro, I'd like very much to hold your hand."

Their fingers interlocked, and a peaceful contentment filled his soul. Climbing the hill, a rising concern crossed Frank's mind.

How am I going to tell Arthur about this?

TEN
For the Fatherland

Lieutenant Hanz Lambrecht stared in disbelief as the motorized column sped north along the country road. Just two weeks earlier, everyone had been in a good mood and eager to see action. The pre-invasion spell of uncertainty and waiting had snapped at last. *But to be displaced by this enemy so quickly?* Now, they scurried north toward Lyon with their swastikas tucked firmly between their legs.

The images still flashed in his mind.

Earlier that afternoon, officers moved into a warehouse near railroad tracks. Their unit was one of several defense lines meant to hold Allied forces in an effort to buy time for the rest of the army group. A 40mm gun emplacement on a knoll overlooked the building the officers met in and seemed to offer protection.

But American fighter planes buzzed low through the air and strafed. A hail of bullets sent soldiers diving for cover. Company Leader Fankhauser, walking the lane near the tracks, was killed instantly. Privates Roush and Maierhofer, alone in a shack where the signalman must have stayed, put their barracks bags against a window, probably to keep any light from escaping when it darkened.

The first three bombs missed.

One of the planes circled around for a second pass and dropped a fourth, fifty yards from that railroad crossing. The concussion from the blast was so great, it blew glass from the window through the barracks bags and killed both. That ambush from the air, in addition to everything the last fourteen days, told the lieutenant something. This enemy, the *Amerikaner*, were ones the Germans had never encountered before.

Lambrecht leaned into the car seat and rested his weary head. He let out the kind of long breath that conveyed something between hope and despair.

Private Schmidt guided the gray-speckled Volkswagen along the bumpy road. Behind the four-piston command car, a column of armored cars, half-tracks, and German soldiers meandered along the dirt road.

Pffft, pfft, pffft!

Suddenly, spouts of fire flicked along the column and splashes of dust staccatoed the road. Bullets rained everywhere.

Vehicles slammed to a stop, and soldiers scattered in every direction.

In a blur, fighter planes screamed over the column.

Lambrecht's attention shot skyward. *Americans again!*

A driver and two German officers piled out of the car in front and scattered for neighboring fields.

Hanz leapt from his car. Several vehicles farther back in the column burst instantly into orange-and-red flames. In an effort to move quickly, Hanz's driver, Schmidt, tripped over a dropped rifle, lost his balance, and fell.

Lambrecht scrambled back to the young private, grabbed an arm, and pulled him into the shelter of a stone wall. Without warning, the car they'd driven in seconds earlier exploded. The heat from the flames rocketed in all directions, but the two men lay untouched.

"Don't move!" Lambrecht shouted.

If soldiers were dazed before, they were terrified now. Another armored vehicle erupted in the procession. Private Schmidt ducked on reflex. A small fireball billowed to the heavens, and a concussion of sound hit the men like a punch in the face. Screams, bullets, and bombs littered the air. Bodies of men he had breakfasted and shared stories of home with burned in vehicles they could not escape.

It would be more humane to just shoot them than let them burn. Lambrecht cursed the war. For a split second, thoughts of Liechtenstein and home surfaced. But being an officer for Hanz was much like playing poker. Every expression, every gesture must exhibit confidence. He could show no fear or indecision.

The strafing and bombing continued another five minutes. It might as well have lasted five hours.

After fifteen minutes of terror, the planes vanished into the clouds and were gone. Bodies emerged from grass fields, beside the wall, and behind trees. Soldiers drifted back to the train of fire, pale and shaky. Lambrecht wondered how so many survived the rain of bullets.

Had this been a sign of things to come? A decision had to be made. *This opponent is different.* Lambrecht and the other officers took an inventory of the destroyed vehicles and equipment.

Colonel Freidrich Richter's slim form paced between the column and stone wall with small quick strides. A pencil-thin mustache no wider than the base of his nose provided the illusion of no upper lip when he spoke. "Lieutenant!" He marched directly at Hanz, boiling with impatience. "Your thoughts. *Now*!"

Lambrecht tilted his head skyward, checking for any sign of this relentless enemy. "While time is of the essence, I believe it prudent to wait."

"*Wait*? How long?"

A putrid odor of burnt vehicle and flesh hung thick in the air. Smoke poured from the nearest half-track. Two soldiers, one's arm burned to the bone, lay near the hedgerow and moaned in pain.

It's too dangerous in the open!

"Till darkness..." Lambrecht hesitated at the chaos surrounding him. "And then, under its cloak, we make for Lyon. Over there..." Pointing a finger, he indicated. "Farmhouses. There and over there. Camouflage the vehicles. Some can hide in the barn, others along this stone wall. The men get a deserved rest, and we gather our thoughts."

The colonel nodded in agreement and threw back his head. "Hoffman!"

The private standing near the column slung his SIG 44 assault rifle over his shoulder and lumbered toward the officers. His *Stahlhelm*, or "steel helmet," bounced along the way.

Lambrecht bit his lip to hide his frustration. *How young is this soldier standing in front of me? A boy of? Sixteen?*

The private straightened his *Stahlhelm*, revealing tight blond curls. "*Jawohl!*"

And ready to die for the Fatherland.

"I am postponing the march. Vehicles are to be hidden in dense bushes or in nearby barns," the colonel declared.

Lambrecht nodded as if hearing the command for the first time and not having offered insight.

"We will continue under protection of darkness," the colonel continued.

"*Jawohl. Heil Hitler.*" Hoffman spun on his heels and spread the word.

*****

Thirty minutes later, Lambrecht rested inside the snug confines of a quaint farmhouse kitchen. The interior of the structure was plain and sparse. Freshly hewn timbers lined one of the walls; a cupboard covered most of it. *Perhaps...a repair?* A small plate of cheese, loaf of bread, and pot of coffee sat on the side of a plain wooden table, around which he and three other officers sat. Spread between them, a map of France covered most of the table.

A farmer and his wife stood next to a stove in the corner. Undoubtedly, they offered servitude and prayed for mercy. A small stack of firewood lay on the floor next to the elderly couple. The old woman opened the cupboard and gathered a set of dishes. Her wrinkled hands trembled as she set the table. Like peasants of the earth, these humble creatures took no more than they needed to survive. But Lambrecht knew, with a man like Richter in charge, their survival was doubtful.

A plate shattered on the wooden floor boards.

"You are quite sure they do not speak German?" the colonel asked Lambrecht.

"To the best of my knowledge, no."

"Tell her, if she and her husband do as we say, they have nothing to fear. We'll be gone by sunset." Richter smiled reassuringly, revealing crooked teeth.

Lambrecht turned to the couple, noticed a wooden crucifix hanging on the wall, and spoke in a calm, reassuring tone. He smiled for effect. The poor couple managed a feeble nod and continued to make themselves busy.

Turning back to the table, Hanz examined the officers near him. One colonel, two captains, and himself. Hoffman, the private, nephew to Richter, stood outside the closed door. Lambrecht's invitation to the table was due to his knowledge of anything French. But Hanz also knew Richter favored him. Early in the war, Hanz acquired key information from locals that resulted in a seizure of weapons and valuables. He had shared the intelligence with Richter who later received an accommodation. Richter promised Hanz a quick advancement through the German ranks, and since then, respected his opinion greatly. Still, Richter relished the opportunity to *give* orders and hold the occasional appearance of a tyrant, much like the *Führer* himself.

The colonel, eyes as gray as the watered coffee from which he sipped, cleared his throat. "Where are the Panzers?"

Captain Adler, barrel-chested and with an aggressive air, crossed his arms. "The 11th Division is near Montélimar. It will be days before we see them."

"The *Amerikaner* attack from behind. The Allies attack our flanks." A sense of dread lay in the colonel's next words. "Like a pack of wolves that never stray far."

"Can we expect support from the *Luftwaffe*?" Captain Kruger asked.

"*Nein,*" Richter replied. "From what I understand, they are as scattered as we."

"And our communication with them quite limited," Lambrecht added.

Kruger's ascetic face rested on top of a thin neck and lean body. He was a beanpole of a man and wore his officer's cap low on his forehead, covering a sparse tuft of wiry blond hair. No matter where he moved, light never hit below his forehead, giving the constant appearance of dark and beady eyes. He reached for the plate of food. *How fitting...the rat goes for his cheese.*

"We have lost Marseille and Toulon." A piece of brie flew from Kruger's mouth.

Richter pounded both fists onto the table. "*Verdammt!*" A beige coffee cup crashed to the floor, and liquid splashed the men's boots. Richter snapped his fingers at the woman. "Clean this! *Now!*"

She tore the apron from her waist, fell to her knees, and patted the liquid. Apparently, no translation was needed. Her husband picked up shards of ceramic cup and set them to the side.

"Tell me what I do *not* know!" Richter roared.

Lambrecht turned his attention from below the table to the colonel, his boots untouched by the spilled liquid. "Soon the 11th will race north to fill their objective as a defense shield. Montélimar is lost."

The only sound heard was the apron dabbing the floor. Richter glanced down and screamed, "*Enough!*"

Body shaking, she jumped to her feet and joined her husband in the corner.

"Our main lines..." Lambrecht's finger pounded the map. "Whether they are here or *here*, must go through Lyon. I believe Army Group G will establish a stable defense line, but it won't be until...here." He pointed again to the map.

"My God, the Americans push from the west and Russians from the east." Captain Adler uncrossed his arms and leaned into the table. "We'll be suffocated."

"Unless..." began Lambrecht. He held everyone's attention. "We must slow their advance as much as possible. Only then can we hold the enemy at bay, regroup, and counterattack. I know for a fact new armament is on the way. All is certainly not lost."

"*Yes!*" Richter shouted. "We will destroy all bridges, railroads...even highways. Send small groups of soldiers for nighttime warfare to slow the enemy at all costs." He turned to his lieutenant. "What can we expect in the form of French resistance?"

"Light and scattered," Lambrecht replied.

Not much different from our resistance.

Richter's cheeks reddened, and a vein bulged in his forehead. Without warning, he thrust his legs back against the chair and stood straight. Wooden chair legs screeched across the wooden floor. He strutted to the window, where the setting sun lit his form in a strange glow, making him appear even more infuriated.

"The sun is setting." His words were lifeless, like a slab of cold marble. After a pause, he grinned. "Give the order. We move out in ten minutes."

Captain Adler sprang from his seat. *"Jawohel! Heil Hitler!"* The door creaked on its hinges then slammed behind his exit.

The colonel folded the map neatly and slid it inside his left coat pocket. He took one last sip from a beige cup then reached for a piece of cheese, plopped it into his mouth, and bit down. Striding to the door, he paused.

With one foot outside the wooden frame, he looked over his shoulder at the farmers and smiled. "Lieutenant..." Richter's glare, as dull as pewter, revolved toward Lambrecht's. "We need to make a lasting impression of German superiority. They are French Jews, are they not?" Richter's voice was metallic and cold, laced with arrogance. He chuckled wickedly. "Shoot them." His crooked teeth, cast inside a crooked smile, spread across an Aryan exterior. "Shoot them both."

Lieutenant Lambrecht nodded behind a poker-faced stare. Kruger followed Richter, and the door closed behind them. Lambrecht pulled his Luger pistol out of its holster and motioned for the couple to stand together. Color drained from their wrinkled faces. They turned to each other and embraced. The old man kissed his wife on her cheek and whispered into her ear. Staring only into each other's eyes, they smiled weakly.

"Für das Vaterland," Lambrecht mumbled. Without blinking, he pulled the trigger seven quick times.

He leaned to the table and, with one quick breath, blew out the candle. Their two forms lay in darkness. Emerging from the house, he tugged an immaculate white handkerchief from his top pocket and wiped his pistol.

For the Fatherland.

ELEVEN
Sunflowers

Sitting at the kitchen table, Frank watched her crack eggs into a frying pan. The smell of toasted bread hung in the air. He sipped black coffee, breathed in its aroma, and exhaled. Neither said a word, but they were acutely aware of each other's presence. Warmth from the cup seeped into his fingers, offering a simple but wonderful comfort, especially in war. This was the most content he had been in a very long time.

An open window allowed sunlight and morning air to stream through. It engulfed Caro.

That same aura hung about her when she sang. Could that have been just yesterday? Frank leaned into his chair and stared. Caro's form exuded a glow and grace possessed only by women, a kind of feminine charm that mesmerizes men and makes them fall abruptly in love for the littlest of reasons.

Held spellbound, he forced himself to remember every detail, knowing in the back of his mind these memories would soon be needed. The way her slender form curved downward. The way her weight shifted between bare feet. She tossed a strand of hair from her eyes with the back of her hand while holding a spatula. Her head tilted as she quietly hummed to herself while cooking breakfast. All etched into his mind.

She had her back to him, but Caro peeked over her shoulder.

"What?" he asked playfully.

"You're staring."

"I just want to remember everything about this morning...about last night."

This dream is about to end.

But he forced that thought to the back of his mind. *Saying four simple words out loud would break this magical spell.* And while, *I have to leave* must pass from his lips, the refusal to acknowledge that fact a little longer kept his reverie intact. Instead, he focused on the bouquet of roses sitting inside a glass vase at the center of the table and inhaled deeply.

They were the flowers he had picked, and he smiled in a self-satisfied way. A postcard leaned against a glass vase in the center of the table. Frank snatched it. The card pictured La Ciotat's beautiful bay on the front. Remembering the story of "secret information" being passed on, he wondered if efforts with the French Resistance had filtered to Caro. He turned the card over.

Three words were scrawled on top. "Dear Aunt Sissel." *I believe they most certainly have.* He leaned the postcard against the vase.

Eggs sizzled on the cast-iron pan. "That sound, that smell..." Frank began. "That's the sound I heard every morning on the farm." He stood and went to Caro's side. The aromas made Frank's mouth water. "After Grandfather and I milked cows, we'd walk into the house, and Grandmother would always fry eggs for breakfast."

Caro flipped the bubbling eggs and stared into the pan.

"You'd think I'd be sick of them, considering what the army does to them." His arms wrapped about her waist, and his chin rested on the top of her shoulder. A faint scent of lavender emanated from her hair. Frank knew, that from now on, whenever he smelled lavender, he would think of her.

"Even though a farm's hard work, it's honest and feels good. But this..." He kneaded her shoulder blades. "Feels better."

"Do not distract the cook." She raised the spatula as if to threaten. "Or I may burst your eggs."

"Hmmm." Frank chuckled playfully. "Sounds dangerous." Raising hands in surrender, he returned to the chair.

A faint smile crossed her lips as she plated the food and set it before him. "We are out of bread. I'll go to Aunt's bakery this morning."

"Let's walk through town after breakfast and go together."

"Ahhh, you want to see the beauty of La Ciotat," she said.

Frank reached for her hand and kissed the top of it. "I already have."

On this morning, the town showed a few signs of life. People moved freely as if awakened from winter's slumber. While there was no evidence of bombings in La Ciotat, a hush of loss and despair had blanketed the town. But whispers of a German retreat conveyed the long-awaited hope. *Libération!*

A group of small children raced past Frank and Caro, playing in the streets.

"These streets are a maze." Frank laughed.

A small, elderly woman built like a broomstick struggled behind a wooden cart, wheeling it onto the cobblestone street. Its limited variety sat on top of a weathered, wooden plank and lit the sidewalk with just enough color. A few lemons and apples huddled in individual rows rested next to some pink wildflowers.

Caro approached the old woman. "*Deux pommes s'il vous plaît.*" She dropped a few coins into a wrinkled, outstretched palm. Caro returned and handed an apple to Frank.

"*Merci.*" Frank bit into the red apple, and juice dribbled onto his chin.

They were strolling arm in arm when a woman hurriedly crossed to the opposite side of the street. "See that woman?" Caro pulled Frank close.

"The one dressed completely in black?"

"*Oui*. She never smiles. She's in perpetual mourning."

"What happened?"

"Her oldest son, James, was a member of the French Resistance and captured by the Gestapo for trying to blow up a German ammo dump. He was tortured and killed. Or at least, that's the story I heard."

"No wonder she mourns."

"Weariness lines her face now...always."

They walked into the shadow of a general store. "I'll be right back." Caro tried to loosen her arm, but Frank's grip held firm. He pulled her close to feel her warmth and stare into her eyes.

She looked at him with a playful gleam. "*Oui?*"

"They say a person's eyes are windows to their soul."

"Then what do you see in my soul, Frank Taylor?"

"I see *happiness*."

"Yours?" She giggled. "Or mine?"

"Hopefully"—Frank pecked her cheek and released her—"both of ours." He stared as her graceful form turned and bounded to the store's entrance. Raven hair bounced on shoulder tops with each step. Peeking back, she flashed a coy smile.

Frank's attention turned behind him, to a lifeless outdoor café on the opposite side of the street. A single bird, a nightingale, perched on a streetlight, chirped away as it soaked in morning light. Black wrought iron chairs sat below the bird, empty and still. *Will life ever return to what it was like? Before the war?*

Caro emerged from the store, sliding a postcard into her pocket. "So..." She bit into her apple. "What do you think, Frank Taylor?"

"What do *I* think?" Frank struck a pensive pose and peeked at the sky. Billowing clouds crawled across the horizon. "I *think* I could live in a place like this."

Her violet eyes widened in surprise. "I thought you wanted your own mountain?"

"Land is good. But the more I think about it, what I really need is time. Time to live. Time to enjoy. Time to grow crops or build a barn. Fix things that are broken."

Caro reached out and straightened Frank's collar.

He leaned to her ear and breathed, "Caro, please don't think I take what we shared last night lightly." A breeze stirred a strand of her hair against her delicate nose. "From the moment I first saw you, I knew."

"And *what* did you know?" Caro leaned in, a breath from his lips.

I must tell her.

His gaze tumbled to the apple he dropped and the gray cobblestone beneath his feet. "Caro, I must leave...this afternoon, with your brother. I don't know what this war holds for me, but when it ends, if my lungs are filled with breath..." Frank gently put his arms around her and drew her close. "I *will* find you."

A sea-born breeze swept over the couple and through the street.

"And I'll be here." Caro tucked dancing hair behind her ears and spoke in a whisper. "I'll be here, waiting."

For a moment, they leaned into each other, pressed cheek to cheek. Frank's hands moved to her face and framed it. He held her and drew her in for a kiss.

Caro pulled back. "You hear me, Frank Taylor? I'll be here. Just don't take your time."

Frank nodded. "My grandfather once told me, 'Time is a thief with many hands.'"

"Then, if that's true, we're born with one hand already in our pockets."

An aroma of freshly baked bread wafted tantalizingly close.

"Come, we're almost there." Caro grabbed Frank's hand and coaxed him past another shop and through the entrance of a bakery. A plump woman with a smudge of flour on her chin and an immaculate apron covering her wide form stood behind the counter. "*Tante* Margaret!"

Margaret shoved a half-filled cookie sheet into a display case and threw her arms open. "*Ma chérie!* You look well!" Two quick kisses and a strong embrace greeted Caro.

Uncle Jean trudged from the kitchen, wiping hands on an already-dirty apron. Dark, thinning hair scattered his forehead, and his wide form shuffled past the counter. "I hear my lovely niece!"

"Uncle!"

"How is my *belle* on this sunny morning?"

"Wonderful! *Merci,* Uncle Jean."

Caro glanced at Frank and pulled him by her side. "I have someone I'd like you both to meet. This is Frank. He's American and visiting with Arthur."

"Ohhh, *Américain*!" squealed Aunt Margaret. "Very pleased to meet you."

"The pleasure is mine, ma'am," Frank said.

"Margaret..." Uncle Jean eyed the kitchen. "We have a tray of fresh—"

"Baguettes!" Aunt Margaret interrupted. "Caro, come help! Like old times, I give you first pick!" She waddled past the counter and into the kitchen, Caro trailing behind. Margaret's shrill voice echoed from the kitchen. "This *Américain* is most handsome!"

Uncle Jean wiped both hands on his apron and eyed Frank. "You are the one who brought Arthur home."

"Yes, sir."

"He visited late last night. *Merci* for bringing him home. We talked much about the war. He spoke very highly of you."

"Thank you, sir."

"I also see my niece is quite taken with you."

"She's a very special young woman."

Reaching into a display, he grabbed a croissant and extended it toward Frank. "Hungry?"

"No, sir."

The portly baker pulled the roll back and nibbled on a corner. "Give a man a roll, feed him a day, but teach a man to bake?" Uncle Jean set the roll onto the countertop and patted his stomach. "Frank, how well do you know my niece?"

Frank cleared his throat, almost choking on his saliva. "*Sir*?"

"Do you know Caro's favorite flower?"

"No, sir," Frank stammered. "I don't. Roses?"

Uncle Jean shook his head. "Well, I do."

Frank waited for the answer. "And?"

"*And*, there's a floral shop at the end of this street that just happens to sell sunflowers."

"Sunflowers?"

"Oui."

"*Merci,* Uncle Jean! I'll be right back."

He bolted out the door and jogged to the street corner. A floral scent led him into the shop. Frank swore the same freshness lingered in the night air on Grandfather's farm. His eyes scanned shelves until he found a bouquet of fresh sunflowers tucked between red pansies and purple lilacs. Reaching into his pocket, he pulled out an American dollar and pointed at the sunflowers.

"All of them. I'll take all of them. They are perfect." The woman's eyes lit at the sight of an American dollar. She reached greedily into the bucket and pulled the entire bunch, still dripping with water. "*Merci*." Frank stepped outside and spun in the direction of the bakery.

Pop! Pop! Pop!

Frank recognized the sound immediately. Three gunshots shattered the morning air.

Screams erupted.

Stunned, Frank stood in the street and watched two men pile into a waiting car. One jumped into the front seat behind the steering wheel. The other into the back, pulling another figure.

"Frank!"

Her blood-curdling shriek struck him like a whip. Staring in disbelief, Frank's legs began to stride.

The figure thrashed in the back seat. "Frank!"

Everything went numb as Frank's legs fell into a sprint.

"*Frank!*"

A haze surrounded his mind, and everything slowed to a torturous crawl. Every hair on his neck and spine electrified. Only one thing mattered. "*Caro!*"

"Fran—"

The man in the back smashed her across the mouth with a closed fist, and she collapsed.

Frank gained on the car, but the man glanced back, and upon seeing him, screamed at the driver. "*Gehen! Gehen!*"

Frank ran so fast, he nearly toppled over.

Car wheels spun with abruptness, spitting gravel. Frank extended arms. Fingertips. Every fiber in his body strained for the bumper.

The man in the rear seat stared back with an icy glare.

For a moment, Frank's eyes locked onto his. *His eyes! One is blue and the other...brown!*

The blond-haired man glanced down at Caro then back at Frank, and smiled wickedly. Pulling just out of grasp, the vehicle accelerated. The man in the back seat delivered a Nazi salute, grinned, and mouthed, "*Heil Hitler.*" The car cleared the first hill then the one after that and disappeared north.

Breathless, Frank stumbled forward, doubled over, hands on knees, everything scrambled in his world. Out of the corner of his eye, Frank glimpsed the yellow bouquet, still held in his hand. *The bakery!*

Pivoting toward the shop, his strides carried him there in seconds. Not stopping at the entrance, he dashed inside and found a broken form lying on the ground. Aunt Margaret knelt at Jean's side, wailing. His body lay motionless, his apron soaked with blood. "We need to put pressure on it!" But Frank knew she was hysterical and did not understand a single word. He grabbed the apron from around her neck and fell to his knees. Frank balled the cloth and pressed, applying direct pressure onto the spurting wounds. His mind raced to make sense of a world turned upside down.

Arthur's voice echoed from outside. "*Ma Tante! Mon Oncle!*" He scampered through the doorway and froze.

Frank glanced from his knees. "Arthur, *go!* Get help!"

With terror in his eyes, Arthur nodded and flew from the shop.

Margaret's wailing dissolved into sobs. Despite the creeping doubt in Frank's mind, he tried to voice reassurance. "Jean! Stay with me! You're going to be all right... Jean!" Frank pressed against the man's side when he noticed his own sticky hands, warm and blood-soaked. A world of death and violence struck a familiar chord in Frank's mind. And then, horror.

Caro...why? Vivid images tore through his mind like razors until he forced them out.

On the ground, the body seized and a raspy gasp emanated. "Leee..."

Frank leaned to Jean's blue lips and strained to hear. But sound broke into a throaty gurgle. Breath came in ragged gasps. A grimace of pain bolted through Jean's face as his bloody hands clutched Frank's, squeezing the saturated apron.

Eyes flickered wide, and, again, sound trembled from his mouth. "Leee..."

"What're you trying to say?" Frank shook his head rapidly. "I don't underst—"

"Leee...own. Caro. *Leee own.*"

Moments earlier, his wife's white apron had hung from her neck as they prepared for another day of baking. Her once-immaculate cloth, her shield of protection, now pressed desperately against her husband's wounded side.

His body stilled.

Next to the outstretched body, blood flowed thickly across the floor. The sweet, sickening smell pierced Frank's nostrils, and a wave of nausea rushed over him. Turning his head to the side, he gasped a quick breath. He glanced at the countertop and caught sight of a bitten croissant. All he thought, over and over again, was one word.

Why?

Inch by inch, blood oozed across the cold floor. The color of life, and death, neared the scattered bouquet, and Frank watched helplessly as the broken sunflowers became drenched in blood.

TWELVE
Miracle

When bullets pierced absolute darkness, Michael had no time to react, no time to think, no time to breathe. Seven consecutive *pops* immediately followed by seven splintered holes inches from his chest. *My God...*

Reflexively, hands rose to his torso, feeling for any wound or warm flow of blood. But there was none. Moments before, muffled German voices argued only feet from his hiding place. All that separated them was a thin, wooden wall. Frozen in the alcove, Michael waited and did the only thing he could, listen.

Silence. Darkness. *What is going on?* Thoughts raced to Albert and Geneviève. *Please, God. Please let them be okay.*

An hour ago, they had been preparing dinner when a barking dog warned something was different. Not only was it different but terribly wrong. A German motorized column approached with more soldiers than Albert could count.

Michael had scampered for the bedroom and into the closet. Falling onto his knees, this time oblivious to pain, he pushed boots aside, opened the cubbyhole, and climbed through. Once inside, he stood and shuffled halfway down the corridor. Geneviève closed the door and concealed the entrance. Trapped between walls, breathing stale, hot air, he could hear the motorcade approach.

And then, all hell broke loose. Bombs exploded, guns fired, even screams shattered the air. *Are the Germans being attacked?* Second after torturous second passed.

Albert's stern voice passed through the thin wall. "Don't move."

Sweat dripped into Michael's eyes, rolled down his back, and soaked his shirt. The next sounds were German voices. *German voices inside the house!* They seemed confused, perhaps even concerned, but always so dangerous. Michael waited for discovery of the hidden passage, to be held at gunpoint and thrown onto his knees. *My God, I'm going to be executed.* His mind raced.

And then...gunshots. Seven streaming rays of light illuminated the darkness right next to him. Then complete darkness. He waited.

And waited.

Engines eventually roared to life. *Did the column continue its march*? The noise diminished and disappeared. Michael did not know how long he stood.

Candlelight flickered to life.

Shuffling toward the holes, he peeked through splintered wood. A candle burned on the kitchen table. Then a sound emanated just outside the cubbyhole. Michael considered sliding to the other end of the corridor and fleeing to the barn. And while he knew the small door in the closet could be opened, seeing into the alcove was another story. *Unless someone knows I'm here.* His heart pounded as if it would burst. The door creaked open, and a tunnel of light cast onto the floor at the closet end, six feet from where he stood. Sweat dripped into Michael's burning eyes, and a soaked sleeve wiped it away.

"Michael?" It was Albert's voice. "Come. It's safe now."

Michael shuffled to the light, dropped to his knees, and crawled through the opening, praying the Gestapo was not on the other end. He looked up from his knees and stammered, "G-Geneviève?"

*****

Michael sat at the kitchen table across from Albert. The old man stared into the candlelight, a look of incredulity spread on his face. Shards of ceramic remains lay on a countertop to the side of the stove. Michael looked below the tabletop and noticed a damp wooden floor. *Had something spilled?*

Geneviève opened the cupboard and pulled out a coffee cup. Placing it on the table, she reached behind her to the stove and grabbed a steaming coffeepot. She filled each of their three cups and sat next to her husband. Albert placed an arm around his wife's shoulders and pulled her in. She nuzzled her head against his shoulder.

Michael leaned forward in his seat and swallowed. "What happened?"

"After you hid, column was attacked by *Américains*. Fearing their safety, Germans hid in our barn, along wall, under trees, and neighbors' barns. Our house became meeting room for officers," Albert said.

Amazed at the thought, Michael's jaw dropped. "There *were* German officers on the other side of the wall." *In this very house!* "Do you know what they said?"

"No. But they argued over a map. Were concerned."

A slow smile spread winningly on Geneviève's face. "Because they run in fear."

"How many officers were there?" Michael asked.

"*Quatre,*" the farmer said. "And one German spoke perfect French."

Geneviève nodded. "One with clean boots."

"This officer was not in...what's the word?" Albert looked at his wife, shrugged, and blurted, 'command?'"

Geneviève raised a finger and pointed at her teeth.

"Ahhh...*oui.* One officer in command had mouth of crook—" Albert's teeth gritted together.

"Crooked teeth!" Michael exclaimed.

"*Oui.* After they argue over map. Sun started to set. They leave. But one with crooked teeth..." Albert's hand gripped the handle on his coffee mug until his knuckles turned white. "He gives order."

Geneviève turned her head to the side and spat in complete disdain. "*Fils de pute!*"

"Agreed. He ordered officer who spoke French to..." Albert's eyes widened in amazement. "To shoot us!"

"*But how*?" Michael asked. "How are you alive?"

"After everyone left, he alone stood...there." The farmer pointed a few feet from where he sat. "Motioned us to stand together...here. Officer pulled gun out and aimed. We stood in each other's arms, prayed, and prepared to die. But then—"

Geneviève blurted in a rapture of wonder. "A miracle!"

Albert nodded, a thin smile on his lips. "We stand there, and he whispers in French."

"*He whispered? In French?*" Michael leaned to the edge of his seat, all pain in his back forgotten. "What did he whisper?"

"He said, 'Lie on ground. Don't move. Wait one hour.'" Albert's voice trailed off, and his gaze fell to the candlelight. "And then he said something I will never forget."

"What did he say?"

"He said..." The farmer turned to his wife, who finished his thought.

"God be with you."

Michael slumped into his chair, shaking his head in disbelief.

Albert's eyes widened in amazement. "He pulls trigger seven times, spoke a few words of German, blew out candle, and left, closing door behind."

Geneviève dabbed the corner of her eye with a sleeve. "*C'était un miracle.*"

"Agreed." Albert nodded. "The shots hit there." His thin finger pointed to the wooden wall next to the cupboard.

"He missed you, on purpose. But *why*?" Frank stood and walked to the cupboard's edge. "I was behind *here*." His fingertip touched the cupboard. "The bullets struck there." Studying the distance between where he stood and where the bullets pierced the wall, he estimated a distance of no more than half a foot. *Six inches!* It was the difference between life and death.

"After almost an hour, we stood. Geneviève lit candle, and I come to get you."

Michael raised his finger, placed it into one of the splintered holes, and traced. "I can't begin to understand. Why? *Why* would he do this?" His hand fell to his side, and he turned, staring at the couple. "It truly is a miracle."

"Miracles don't need explained." Albert's voice rang with belief. "They are an act of God."

Inside a three-foot space of the alcove, seven rays of light pierced the darkness. Beacons of brilliancy shone through like some bridge spanning reality and illusion. Six inches from where the American once stood, directly behind the embraced couple, seven auras shone like stars in the night.

And if one looked carefully or bothered to notice, they would understand their significance. The constellation is called the Plough.

THIRTEEN
War Is Hell

The same kitchen that rang with song and laughter less than twenty-four hours ago now sat in silence. Arthur pulled his bedroom door closed, trudged to the kitchen table, and slumped into a chair. Both he and Frank, now in uniform, stared into nothingness.

Frank inhaled slowly, as if the air itself was comprised of sorrow.

A vase of roses rested between them. They were the flowers Frank had picked for her. A brownish tinge had already faded onto the petals' edge and begun its slow creep to the heart of each blossom. It would not be long before the flowers browned completely, withered, and died.

Frank's mind raced with images of Caro, sunflowers, Germans, and blood. He tried to focus, for soldiers' lives depended on him. *Perhaps, if I refuse to think her name.*

But that was impossible. Wave after wave of regret washed through his tortured soul.

Frank glanced at his fingernails revealing nothing but cleanliness. Every speck of blood scrubbed away. Of all possible images of Uncle Jean, only Frank's bloodstained hands could be envisioned. "We need to get back."

Arthur nodded.

Frank leaned forward as if to stand, but the fading rose petals held his gaze. Reaching out, he snapped off one of the blooms and tucked the rose into his left shirt pocket. Noticing the postcard leaning against the vase, he grabbed and pocketed it as well.

There was no engulfing brightness when they emerged from the house. A gray haze hovered oppressively low over an equally gray sea. From a distance, it was impossible to distinguish one from the other. It seemed to Frank the dull drain of war had seeped into sea, sky, and even the flowers. The golden air of yesterday was gone, and the prevailing lack of variety matched the sergeant's mood perfectly.

Arthur locked the front door, ambled down the stone steps, and looked over his shoulder at the house of his boyhood, perhaps for the final time. He shook his head and jumped into the passenger side of the Jeep. Frank peeked at his friend, but, not knowing quite how to express his shared grief, turned the ignition, and the vehicle roared to life. Grinding into gear, the Jeep lurched forward.

The vehicle zigzagged through streets as the men sat in silence. Frank decided to let his friend initiate conversation as he wrestled with his own conscience.

Finally, when well out of town, Arthur spoke. "My uncle was a good man. A *very* good man."

Images of bloody hands flashed in Frank's mind.

"My aunt's a strong woman. But this? It will be quite...difficult." Drawing a heavy breath, he rubbed the dark stubble on his face. "But why? Why my sister?"

"I don't know," Frank replied.

Arthur's hands dropped to his lap. "We may never know."

"I've been trying to make sense of it."

"Tell me again. What did my uncle say to you?"

"He said the words, 'Lee Own.' Then he said Caro's name and the words 'Lee Own' again."

"Lee Own...Lee Own...could he mean the city, Lyon? Lyon, France?" Arthur's gaze darted to his friend. "Do you think he was trying to tell you where?" Nervous glances now held firm.

"But how? How would he know where they took her? Did your aunt tell you anything?" Frank asked.

"She was in the kitchen with Caro pulling bread from the ovens. They heard shouting. First, French voices then German. When she peeked into the front of the store, to make sure everything was okay, two strangers stood in a heated argument with Uncle. The shorter one held a bag of fresh bread while the other, the one yelling, caught sight of Caro and pointed at her." Arthur's eyes narrowed in confusion.

"And then?"

"I don't know. My aunt said everything blurred. Something about the taller one shoving a finger into the other's chest and staring at Caro. He strode to her, grabbed her by the arm, and dragged her outside, to the car. Then, Uncle tried to step in, and they..."

"Arthur, do you think they recognized Caro somehow?"

"Only if they'd been immersed, posing as French citizens for some time."

"Would there be Germans undercover for that long? Here in Southern France?"

"They have spies. We have spies. Pierre told me one was found working in the shipyards just a few miles from here two months ago."

"Pierre?" Frank asked.

"Pierre, a boyhood friend who serves the Maquis. His family lives on the other side of town, by the main shipping yard. Last night was my opportunity to check with old contacts after I visited my aunt and uncle."

Frank's hands jerked on the steering wheel, and the Jeep swerved, avoiding a small crater, the result of some detonation. "You visited them? Last night?"

"After I left you and Caro. We had dinner together. I wanted to say goodbye before we left today," Arthur said quietly.

He glanced at his friend, unsure of his next words.

"All I know is my parents, my uncle, and now my sister..."

Frank patted his friend's shoulder, hoping to offer comfort. "Even if we knew she was on her way to Lyon, there's nothing we can do right now but hope."

"And pray." Arthur rubbed both eyes with the heels of his hands. "Evil truly knows no bounds."

"Nor will justice, when it's delivered." The tires slammed into a hole, and Frank pushed his helmet off his forehead. "Germans *are* retreating north. It's most likely their path will take them through Lyon."

Arthur gazed at a distant tree line on the horizon, his voice hollow. "Before the war, I knew little of this world or much in it. Just simple pleasures. But, now? I have seen its ugliness firsthand, and I may *never* recover." The Jeep bounced along the dirt road and wound down another hill.

Frank cleared his throat. *I have to tell him my feelings for Caro.* But there was dryness in his mouth. The kind he remembered before confession at church. Not sure how to put feelings like this into words, he licked his lips. "Arthur, your sister...I want you to know how much I..." Frank's voice trailed off at the approaching sight. An old man stood not far from the road, bent over an erect shovel handle. "What's going on here?" Brakes whined, and the vehicle slowed to a stop. "I wonder if he needs help."

Frank and Arthur hopped out of the vehicle. The old man wiped his sweaty, bald head with a handkerchief tattered with stains. He stuffed the cloth into his back pant pocket and continued digging. He was as wiry as a pencil. Frank's eyes darted to Arthur in uncertainty. "Why would he be digging out in the open? And in the middle of the day?" Frank noticed the man's patched clothes, and how his frail body did not come close to filling them. The man's eyes were raw and red.

The soldiers walked to a pile of dirt and a small heap of straw. It was all that separated the three men.

Flies and an odor of death filled the air. Frank and Arthur peered over the top of the pile. Their shoulders slumped at the sight. On the ground, hidden behind the dirt, were the remains of two bodies.

Consumed by his effort, the old man did not look up. Arthur spoke a few words of French. A small shovelful of dirt hit the pile, and the man paused and mumbled.

Arthur translated. "He says they are his wife and daughter."

The old man mumbled again.

"They were scavenging for food when he heard an explosion behind him."

Again, the man spoke.

"Apparently, they stepped on a mine. He's burying them here because he couldn't..." Arthur's voice cracked. "He couldn't carry what was left to the cemetery."

Frank stared at the remains. *His daughter...probably not much younger than...* But he forced her name from his mind.

The old man muttered a few final words, and the shovel blade dug into the dirt.

Arthur nodded. "*Merci.*" He tugged Frank's sleeve. "Come." Both soldiers returned to the Jeep. "He didn't want our help," Arthur said.

Frank glanced back as the old man threw straw into the hole, a bedding for the grave. "But why? Why wouldn't he want our help?" Frank jumped inside the vehicle and fingered the ignition.

"He says he didn't want us to touch them." Both men stared at each other. "He didn't want us to touch them because..." Arthur paused. "Because he buries his life."

Inhaling deeply, Frank looked back to the old man. He was going to speak but once again could not find the right words.

"There is an emptiness. A hollowness in death." Arthur's voice resonated with sorrow. "It causes one to crawl inside their own clouded heart and never let anyone in."

Frank threw the vehicle into gear, and both soldiers peered one final time. They watched with utter desolation as the old man fell to his knees and wept uncontrollably.

FOURTEEN

On the Run

American Colonel Joe Looby stood in the middle of the structure and let out a low whistle. Realizing the damage that had occurred, even he was impressed. In the middle of the night, half the church's roof vanished as if ripped away by some curious giant's hand. Exploding shells had buckled the east wall and shattered all but one stained-glass window. Shards of colored glass and flakes of red brick blanketed everything inside and crunched under the weight.

Only the altar, with a crucifix perched atop, survived unscathed. Whispers of a miracle would no doubt soon circulate throughout the parish, and the colonel found himself in complete agreement. *At least,* Looby thought, *parishioners' pleas are no longer hindered by man-made construction.* They could now ascend directly to God's ear.

One lone, intact window stood sentinel in the covered half of St. Francis Cathedral. A makeshift American headquarters rested below. Light streamed through the stained glass from outside, faces illuminated in a multitude of colors within. Only Looby seemed to notice the spectrum of colors as he strolled toward the meeting about to commence. Two aides blanketed in diffused yellow light bounced between phones. A radio operator radiating in purple sat next to green-hued desks scattered with papers and a makeshift mailbox containing multiple slots. One staffer, his face lit in blue, pounded on a typewriter while sitting in a splintered church pew. A spotlight of crimson cast onto Major General Derrick Hoover and the officers huddled around him.

Looby stood at the rear of the group and glanced down at his shirtsleeves. Instead of a crimson shade, his clothing lit with a color more inclined toward terracotta.

Hoover studied two vertical maps hanging on the wall. Weathered creases lined the major general's brow like deep furrows in a blood-red field. "We've just decoded a German communique, and I believe an opportunity presents itself. The Germans are retreating into Northern France." Hoover gnawed the end of a cigar. Ash droppings added to an already-littered floor. "German flanks are exposed here." His finger, thick like one of the cigars lining his pocket, pounded a map. "And here, east of the Rhône at Grenoble." The chart rippled beneath his fingertip. "Taskforce Butler will advance, paralleling German evacuation routes. *Lieutenant.*"

Lieutenant General Joseph Bogdan hovered behind Hoover's left shoulder, staring at the maps. Bogdan's alabaster face had a poker-like stare, void of emotion. "Our goal is to beat them to the spot, farther north. Cut them off at the pass so to spea—"

"Exactly!" Hoover wore his olive-drab garrison cap to the side. "The 36th Infantry Division will also continue north while VI Corps pursues from behind." Tufts of smoke-gray hair protruded haphazardly from underneath the sides of his cap.

Brigadier General DeGasperis' soft voice, belying a rugged, bearlike exterior, echoed from Hoover's right. "We need to move with urgency, before their communication is reestablished."

The major general's head rotated to the brigadier general. "What's that?"

DeGasperis cleared his throat and tried again, boosting his voice. "I said, sir, we move with urgency, before their communication is reestablished."

"Damn right! I don't want to stop. I don't want to slow. I want their foxholes to be our foxholes. Understood?" Hoover's gaze clung to the maps before he spun and barked like a quarterback directing a play. "*Understood?*" Broken glass crunched under his boot soles.

"Yes, sir!" resonated from the crimson huddle. All officers nodded in agreement.

"Colonel Looby!" Hoover ripped the gnawed remnants of a cigar out of his mouth and flipped the frayed tobacco toward a trash can. "Your evaluation of the Kraut retreat."

Looby unwound his lanky frame and stood tall. "Roads are crowded, fuels at a premium, and our incessant strafing attacks are forcing them to make most of their movements by night. They are resorting to guerrilla tactics...burning bridges, random attacks. But we can catch them, sir."

"How about their Panzer withdrawal?" the general asked. "They need to cross waterways as well."

"Yes, sir. The number of ferries capable of carrying their forty-five-ton Mark V Panther tanks is limited." Looby pushed forward, squeezed past Hoover's blocklike frame, and connecting a pair of black, break-apart glasses over his nose, examined the map. "They will need to cross the Rhône and move north as quickly as possible to secure a German route of withdrawal."

"One thing concerns me." Hoover's face twisted; a sliver of tobacco dangled from his bottom lip. "We need to keep our supply lines secure. We need to keep feeding the machine."

Again, the officers nodded.

Hoover reached inside his cotton field jacket and pulled a fresh cigar. "It's a race, gentlemen." He bit the tip and spat in the vicinity of a trash can. "If we can outpace their flanks, encircle them before they head north, and form a pocket? They'll never be able to scurry into their German hole."

"Their armies from the west, south, and east"—DeGasperis' gaze tumbled from the yellow-hued map to the floor speckled with broken glass—"are funneling through one city."

Hoover's eyes squinted shut as he threw his head back and cupped his ear. "How's that? Sorry. Bad ear."

Brigadier General DeGasperis cleared his throat. "I said, their armies from the west, south, and east are funneling through one city, sir."

"And that, gentlemen"—the map trembled under Hoover's firm smack—"is where we'll squash 'em. All roads, lead through one place."

Without warning, the major general spun and bulled through the red-hued huddle of senior officers. "Follow me."

Every officer turned and trailed but Looby. He pulled his hands from pants pockets, crossed sinewy arms, and stared at the black spot on the map. His soft voice echoed in the snug confines of the dilapidated church.

"Lyon."

*****

Frank Taylor scanned the soupy horizon as columns of American soldiers drifted north along an inundated countryside. The dank smell of men and oil hung thickly in the air. As soldiers sloshed and artillery rolled through mud, most of the time, verdant farmland, meadows, and pastures stretched for miles. Every so often, a tattered village appeared, or perhaps a worn city. Early in the war, progress was measured in feet. Now, if the Americans were not covering almost twenty miles a day, command was upset.

Fighter planes screamed by intermittently, and the knowledge America controlled French skies comforted Frank. Lines of tanks gleamed in the moisture. Each, like a sleek link in a giant chain, advanced. The military machine pushed its way from the southern coast of France into the interior, liberating communities held for months. Germany was on the run.

Despite cloud cover, the landscape never seemed more vibrant. *War should not be fought in a country as beautiful as this.* The rich and fertile greenness of the meadow reminded Frank of lush Kansas fields. *War should be fought in a country as ugly as war.*

"Sarge, what's the plan?" Haubert pulled the stump of a cigar from his mouth, hawked, and spat on the ground.

"North. Town by town, city by city. We bulldoze these bastards back to their hole."

"Then"—Risaliti shifted the weight of his rifle from one shoulder to the other—"we bury them."

Frank nodded then considered the obvious. The enemy was moving directly toward Lyon. Out of the corner of his eye, he glimpsed Arthur striding next to him. Faint words tumbled from Frank's lips. "Lee Own."

Arthur turned. "Frank?"

"Just thinking about Uncle Jean, Lyon...and—"

"I know. Were his words a reference to the city?" Arthur's fingers swiped raindrops from the beginnings of a thick beard and flicked them to the ground. "These thoughts consume me as well."

A vehicle honked repeatedly from behind, and, as it neared, the men gave way.

Haubert wiped his forehead with a soaked sleeve and placed the butt of his rifle on top of a muddy boot. "Well, I'll be damned."

Piero stared into the parting sea of men. "Who is it?"

"It's the ol' man. The head honcho. The big cheese. None other den Major General Hoover himself." Haubert jerked a thumb in his direction. "Come to give us one of his famous pep talks, no doubt."

The Jeep squealed to a stop, and the men formed a circle around it. Despite the steady drizzle, a smoldering cigar protruded from the general's lips. He stepped from the vehicle and slopped into a puddle of muck. Oblivious to the soaked condition of his boots, Hoover straightened his back and puffed his thick chest like a rooster. He strutted around the vehicle, eyeing the soldiers, before breaking into a fiery tone. "Men...it has fallen upon us to drive the enemy from this land! It has fallen upon us to liberate this country and all of Europe!" Hoover ripped the gnawed cigar from his mouth and spat into the mud. "It has fallen upon us to deliver the world from *Nazi* tyranny! And by God, it *will* be done!"

Moore leaned behind Risaliti and muttered, "The only thing fallen upon us is enemy fire."

"And rain," Risaliti snickered.

Hoover grinned at the men encircling him, eagerness burning in his eyes. "I want to let my men know how damn proud I am of them. It takes a *hell* of a soldier to look evil in the face and stare right back." The general spun to the nearest soldier. "What's your name, son?"

"Mmmy nnname?" The soldier at Hoover's side stood rigid. Piero shot nervous glances at Frank then stared at the major general, mouth agape. "Mmmy nnname?" Words escaped the private's mouth at a level bordering scream. "My name's PFC Piero!"

Hoover's eyes shot open, and he recoiled a step. "Where you from, Private?"

An elbow poked Frank, and he turned to see a catlike grin crossing Risaliti's and Haubert's faces.

"Indiana, sir!"

"Ahhh, you're a Hoosier?"

The PFC yelled into the major general's face. "No, sir!"

Almost every man in Piero's unit shook with contained laughter.

Hoover squinted and he thrust his cigar into the private's chest. "But you're from Indiana?"

"That's true, sir! But I like to consider myself a f-f-fan of the fighting Irish, sir!"

"I like your constitution, son. By God, you seem eager for more action."

"Sir, yes, sir! Time to give those Nazi b-b-bastards hell! Sir!"

A wide smile arched the major general's lips. "The Army needs soldiers like you. You're a go-getter. Now, go and get me some Nazi ass!"

"Thank you! I will, sir! Get you some ass! Lots of Nazi ass, sir!"

"Keep up the good work, Private." Hoover clapped Piero on the back and hopped into the mud-splattered Jeep. The vehicle roared to life, cranked into gear, and sloshed through a sea of parting men and flying brown muck.

After containing laughter for the duration of Hoover's stay, the men finally burst. Howls of hilarity coursed through Taylor's unit. Moore shook his head in disbelief, both eyebrows furrowed high into his forehead. Haubert bent over, choking with laughter. Risaliti patted Piero on the shoulder with vigorous sarcasm. "Z, you're one humdinger!"

"Wwwhat? Wwwhat I do?" Piero threw his arms up in frustration. "But I couldn't remember! I couldn't remember!"

"Couldn't remember what?" Frank asked, suppressing a smile.

"I couldn't remember *which* was his bad ear," Piero exclaimed.

"That's okay, Z. I think you covered it. Had he half an ear, he'd have heard you," Risaliti said.

Once again, artillery squealed to life and the men marched forward. Occasionally, a wooden post with a road sign nailed to it gave some indication of location. When Frank looked up to see the painted black word "Lyon" spread on a white sign pointing north, he nudged the soldier next to him.

A thin smile crossed Arthur's lips, and he nodded. "If she's out there, we'll find her."

FIFTEEN
Almost Home

Michael inhaled, and for a moment, swore he was in Kansas. A distinct odor of wooden rafter beams, stacks of hay, and animal pens blazed familiarly through his nostrils. *This could be Grandpa Luke's barn. Frank and I would be on the bales, racing to the top*. He chuckled at the memory and muttered fondly, "There's no place like home, *or* the feeling of having one." He drifted to the rear of the barn, still caught in a most pleasant daydream.

A stack of dried firewood rested below frayed leather horse harnesses hanging from a rusted nail driven into a wooden beam. Michael snatched a few pieces of split cherrywood and faced the farmhouse.

Despite the danger and uncertainty of war, he had found safe haven with this wonderful couple. He understood with complete certainty their risk, and it frightened Michael every moment he stayed. Though his back still ached, the agony that had coursed throughout his body a few days ago had slowly dissipated. A tolerance of discomfort replaced crippling pain.

He snagged the handle with one hand, yanked the door open, and strode into the kitchen. Geneviève pulled a coffeepot from the stovetop, and handed Michael a towel. He opened a stove lid with it and dropped a piece of firewood inside. The wood crackled to life. Next to the cupboard, he stacked the remaining pieces.

Albert sat in the corner of the small kitchen. Smoke wafted from a handcrafted ivory pipe held firm between his lips. He watched with quiet satisfaction as his wife poured three cups of coffee. Geneviève turned to Michael and handed him a steaming cup. "Sorry, is watered down."

The American shook his head in amazement. "Please, you have nothing to apologize for." Michael sipped and enjoyed the warmth of the heated cup between his palms.

Geneviève returned the pot to the stovetop and glanced at Albert, who nodded. She walked to the cupboard and reached into a drawer, rummaging through until a thin chain with an attached medal dangled from her fingers. She turned and faced Michael. The tremor in her voice matched the shaking of her hands. "We want you to have. Belonged to our son."

"You have done too much already. This is too much." Michael shook his head and glanced at Albert in the corner. "I can't accept—"

"*Please,*" he insisted.

"You must. Your courage much like his." Geneviève dangled the chain as Michael extended his palm. "You carry his spirit now." The silver links piled into the cup of his hand. "It is blessed."

Albert, lips taut on the bit of his pipe, smiled. His chest puffed with an air resembling pride. "It is medal of St. Christopher."

"Patron saint of travelers." Tears welled in Geneviève's eyes. "Will see you safely home."

Overcome with the farmers' generosity, Michael threw arms around Geneviève and held her close. "Both of you, I don't know how I'll ever thank you." He pulled away and peered at Albert. "Someday this war *will* end and, God willing, we'll stay in touch. I'll return to visit. And we'll enjoy great food, excellent conversation..." Michael paused, sentiment then laughter cracking his voice. "And strong coffee." Unsure of how to phrase his next question, he lowered his gaze to the patched work pants he wore. "When you welcomed me into your home, you told me these clothes belonged to your son. Now you honor me with his medal. May I ask, what happened?"

Geneviève tugged at the top rail of a wooden chair and sat. Albert puffed on the pipe one final time and pulled it from his mouth. He leaned forward in his chair, elbows resting on knees. "When Germans first entered our village, they round up men and boys between ages of ten and seventy. All forced to labor. Very hard work. One day, a guard beat an old man for slipping to the ground. Our son, Pierre, stepped in to protect. They shot him. He was twenty-seven."

Michael's face froze, mortified by the story. "I'm so sorry."

Expressionless, Albert stood and walked to his room. When he reappeared, he wore a cap, scarf, and coat. "The old man Pierre tried to protect...was me." He placed a hand on Michael's slumped shoulder. "I'll soon return. Maurice is leader of local resistance. He's true friend."

Michael's gaze fell to the silver chain twisting between his fingers. An image of St. Christopher flashed on one side of the dulled pewter medal. "He'll help me get to my men?"

"*Oui*. It'll be dark soon. Not safe to travel until dark. I return within hour." Albert swung the door open and disappeared.

"Give me." Geneviève grabbed the chain and stood. She moved behind Michael and clasped the links around his neck.

Candlelight danced on the metal. "St. Christopher is..." Michael peered over his shoulder at Geneviève. "Christopher's my middle name."

The links slipped from her fingers and onto his shirt. Geneviève kissed the tight curls on top of Michael's head. "*He* will see you safely home."

*****

Albert kept his promise. Within an hour, the door opened, and the old farmer's familiar figure stepped into the kitchen. At his heels, a taller man entered. He wore ebony slacks, a dark-blue button-down, and a raven overcoat that covered his lanky frame. A Basque beret tilted forward on his acorn-shaped head. Thick hair, shaggy and unkempt and as black as ink, curled below the beret and into one of his dark eyes. He rubbed his hands together as if to warm them.

"This is Maurice. He leads French Resistance in area." Albert removed his coat and scarf and disappeared into his room.

A birthmark the shape of Florida sat on Maurice's left cheek. As he extended a hand, Michael glanced down and noticed the other man's boots. "You like? These belonged to a German once. Now they're mine."

Michael chuckled and shook the other man's hand. "We make do with what is available."

"*Oui*. Not bad for a bunch of thugs and thieves. They say, 'The mark of the Maquis is not just the fight in their hearts, but the German boots worn on their feet.' I'll be escorting you northeast. Your American friends are well on their way to driving the Germans out of our country. And word has been sent. They are expecting us."

"Who?"

"My friends. Once there, we have direct route to American lines."

"Your efforts are most welcome. *Merci*."

"My pleasure."

Geneviève appeared from the corner of the kitchen. In her hands, a small burlap sack bound by a piece of thin leather thread. She handed it to Michael. "For journey."

Again overcome by their generosity, Michael shook his head. He bent down and embraced

Geneviève. "Thank you. I'll never forget you." Michael glanced at the sack. "My flight uniform?"

"No. Too dangerous. That buried in barn. This food and drink."

Michael strode toward Albert, who stood next to the cupboard. He grasped the old man's wrinkled, outstretched hand. "I don't know how to thank you. I don't know where to start."

Albert stared into Michael's eyes. "You start where you begin any journey...with one step."

The men fell together in a tight embrace, eyes shining, emotion brimming. "When this war's over, I *will* find you. Both of you."

Albert's lips, taut around his white pipe, loosened just enough for words to drift through. "And we look forward to that day."

On the wooden wall behind the farmer's head, Michael caught sight of the seven splintered bullet holes. "Six inches..." Extending a fingertip to the holes, he traced a line over the rough-hewn wood, connecting them. *The distance between life and death.*

Michael stepped back, threw the burlap sack over his shoulder, and turned. As Maurice swung the front door open, Michael looked one final time at the couple. "I owe my life to you. Thank you for everything. God bless you both."

Outside, two horses stood ready. The Frenchman adjusted his beret. "Know how to ride?"

"I grew up on a farm." Michael climbed into the saddle and glanced into the dusky night sky. It looked as watered down as the coffee he had grown used to. He undid the leather tie and peeked inside the burlap sack. Inside were wrapped sandwiches, a small canteen, two apples, and a little red purse. Michael opened the purse and shook his head. Tucked neatly inside were 750 francs. The American turned and peered over his shoulder. Inside the house, candlelight danced through the window.

Thank you, my dear friends...for everything.

At the neighboring farm, a dog barked.

"Remember," Maurice said quietly. "Night is our protection...night and silence."

"Understood. I just hope this horse knows English." Michael tied the burlap sack to the horn of his saddle.

Maurice snapped the reins and nodded. "Let's go."

SIXTEEN
Her World

Thompsonville, Kansas—August 1944

On the outside, life in Thompsonville, Kansas, hadn't changed much for Maribeth Taylor. Farms still needed work, children attended school, and a trip into town was a chance to catch up with friends. While other flowers faded this time of year, asters bloomed fully and lined the hills with their starry-shaped purple heads. Meadows and fields were never greener. At night, a million stars winked in the heavens, while bullfrogs lined muddy edges of riverbanks, croaking their approval.

A faint breeze slid under cracked windows, and into her second-floor room. Though she lay in bed, Maribeth's eyes remained open. She'd been awake for hours, just staring at the curtains dancing against the wall. She rolled onto her side and inhaled a light, breezy scent. An image of a vast purple field flashed in her mind, but the throaty chime of the grandfather clock downstairs broke her reverie.

The mother of two considered the hour.

Three a.m.

Sleepless nights were a firm part of her routine. To her left, Lawrence slept soundly. It was no wonder, considering he worked three jobs. His own father, Dominic, too feeble and old, could no longer work his own farm.

A phone rang in the hallway. Its shrill tone pierced the night air. Maribeth lurched upright and flipped the light switch. Her husband didn't flinch. A framed black-and-white photograph of two young, grinning boys climbing a haystack rested on the nightstand next to her. An envelope leaned against the frame. Maribeth stared at the photo and hesitated.

Rrring!

Grabbing the frame and envelope in one motion, she rolled out of bed and stumbled down the dark hallway.

Rrring!

She snatched the receiver, not knowing what to expect. Her daughter-in-law's hushed voice whispered. "Mom, turn on the radio. There's another update."

"Okay. Thank you, honey." Maribeth dropped the receiver onto the hook and bounded down the stairs. Though footsteps echoed on the polished wooden floor, she knew Lawrence would not wake. She clicked on the radio and tapped her foot as the speaker hummed to life. A wooden chair once used to rock her children to sleep rested next to the radio. The chair creaked under her weight. She wrapped her arms around the picture frame, and clung to it as if cradling a newborn. As she rocked, her mind wandered, and drowsy eyes closed.

My boys. My sweet, sweet boys. Memories of her sons had always been vivid. It was as if they still lived and worked on the farm. If they *were* home, they'd probably be raiding the refrigerator right now for a late-night snack. She'd always catch them drinking milk out of the bottle when they thought no one was watching.

Family was her lifeblood. They were her driving force.

Her world.

But recently, these memories were not as familiar. They seemed distant and foreign. It was as if someone had covered them with a blanket. While she could distinguish shapes and forms, nothing specific remained. This terrified her.

Finally, a formal voice crackled to life. Her eyes shot open.

"This is Alan Stevenson in the NBC newsroom in New York. Ladies and gentlemen, all night long, bulletins have been pouring in from London. Allied forces in Southern France not only established a beachhead but have captured the towns of Marseilles, Toulon, and Le Muy. It appears American forces are on the march. From the shores of the Mediterranean, now, well into the interior of France, German forces retreat en masse. Ladies and gentlemen, the Germans retreat under pressure from Allied forces. Though casualties will take dreadful tolls, Allied commanders are hoping they are on the brink of..."

The voice on the radio continued to babble, but Maribeth's mind hung on one word, "casualties." She uncrossed her arms and stared at the photograph in her hands. *How my boys loved the farm! Climbing hay bales, helping their father. How young they were!* Though their very image rested on her lap and registered in her mind, in this particular moment, their faces seemed hazy and unrecognizable.

She panicked.

Her fingers quickly tugged at a letter inside the envelope. She unfolded it and managed a faint smile as she recognized her son's familiar script. Maribeth's gaze pored over the special piece of paper.

June 23, 1943

Dear Mother and Father,

While I can't tell you where I'm currently stationed, I can tell you thoughts of home and family dominate my mind. I do not know Frank's whereabouts, only that he, too, will soon be landing in another country.

I hope Grandpa is doing well. Give him my love and tell him to keep that tractor seat warm for me. When I get home, I would love nothing more than to help him every day. I miss the farm terribly, though, every once in a while, a particular landscape here in Europe reminds me of Kansas.

In your last letter, you told me to be careful. The funny thing about war is that a soldier can only be lucky. Athletic abilities, military techniques, trying to be "careful," or moving fast has nothing to do with who survives and who doesn't. If anything, wish us the best of luck.

The horrors of war are everywhere. There is much to fear on the battlefield, but my deepest fear is that if I return, will I have changed? And if so, will it be for the better or worse? Besides the grim cost on human life, the destruction done to these beautiful countries is appalling. It's as if some inebriated giant stumbled through, leaving crushed towns, villages, and cities in his careless wake. And no matter what governments tell us, I refuse to believe that countries have to fight and that humanity has to die. It is detestable.

I am sorry for rambling, but, like yours, there is much weighing on my mind these days. Again, please give everyone my love. I know better than to tell you not to worry. I love you both and will try my best to write soon.

Your Loving Son,

Michael

Maribeth finished the letter and immediately began reading it again.

Then, she folded the letter and slid it into the envelope. After some time, she leaned forward, clicked the radio off, and climbed the steps. Picking up the receiver, she dialed her daughter-in-law. "Sarah, it's Mother. Thank you. Yes, I heard. I know. I'll talk to you in the morning. Love you." Maribeth set the receiver onto the hook.

Drawing a deep breath, she walked into her room and sat on the edge of the bed. She returned the frame and envelope to the nightstand and stared at her boys. Brushing the photograph with a fingertip, she prayed. *Please, God, watch over my boys and keep them safe.*

The wind stirred, and again she scented the faint aroma of asters spread in the field.

Please give Frank and Michael...the best of luck.

She placed her head on a pillow and stretched out on the mattress. Lawrence snored quietly at her side. Sleep would not come this night. She closed her eyes, but the usual images of school, farm, and family that ran through her mind escaped her. On this sleepless night, her thoughts turned to little pieces of paper.

Mothers of every serving soldier across the United States feared boys on bicycles, for they delivered telegrams to doorsteps. Much of the time, the little pieces of paper began with five dreaded words: *We regret to inform you.* Some of the time, words expressed that a soldier had *disappeared* or been "lost." Either way, these tiny messages delivered the most ominous news a mother could ever receive. *Will tomorrow be my day? The day after?*

And if she received two telegrams? That was unimaginable.

Little paper, little hope.

The only thing she could do was cling to the soft voice deep inside. Though at times just an echo, and very faint, she always held to a maternal belief that her sons were alive, well, and would eventually return home.

Living in Thompsonville would continue, but in her world, life would never be the same.

SEVENTEEN
Prisoner

France —August 1944

Though a burlap sack covered her head, it fit loosely enough to still allow breath. For that, she was thankful. But her wrists and ankles throbbed with shooting pain. Knotted rope bit into hands tied behind her back. Cramps riddled her roped legs. Caro wet her lips. The taste of blood lingered in her mouth, and a side of her face felt puffed, still swollen from being punched.

When the car screeched to a halt, Caro's weight shifted to the edge of the back seat. She pushed her feet against the interior of the car to keep from falling to the floor. She heard car doors open. A pair of strong hands grabbed and tossed her over a shoulder. One of the soldiers muttered to the other. She was no more than a large sack of flour for whoever carried her. As Caro rocked back and forth in the air, despite bound hands, her fingertips slipped into a pocket on the side of her dress. Tugging at the postcard purchased with Frank, she let it slip from her grip.

A door creaked open and despite the darkness, she became aware that whoever carried her entered a building. The footsteps beneath her climbed a staircase. She remained limp, as if unconscious, but her mind never stopped tracking the path her captors took. They ascended a large staircase then another. *Multiple floors.* Painful moans echoed on one level. Strained German voices raced on the next.

Through small holes of the burlap sack, shards of light trickled inside. Caro counted each step but could distinguish nothing else. After about fifty stairs, she was carried down a corridor. A right-hand turn, a few more strides, and her body dumped onto a cot. Feet shuffled from the room, and a door closed. She did not know her location or what would happen next.

But she was alive...on the fifth floor of some building.

Arthur, my dear brother, find me. Muffled German voices chattered just outside the room. *Frank, my sweet, dear Frank. Don't give up on me.*

Caro's heart pounded, and her mind flew to a simple childhood memory. *Speak when spoken to, be respectful, and remember our story.*

She prayed it would be enough.

*****

"Her family is Maquis." The taller man, dressed as a civilian, jerked a thumb in her direction.

"You are certain of this?" asked Richter.

"Quite. We observed her parents for some time. They were of a high level in the resistance and caused many problems for us. That was, until they were eliminated."

"Why was *she* permitted to live?"

"She was but a girl then." Also dressed as a civilian, a shorter man leaned toward the colonel. "And for some reason, on that night, could not be found. When she resurfaced, our orders were only to observe and blend into the community."

"I don't have time for these petty concerns. The Maquis are nothing more than thugs and thieves. Our stay is quite temporary. We move out early morning, on to Dijon. Eliminate her."

"But, Colonel, we brought her to you because we thought..." A wry smile escaped the taller man's lips. "You should enjoy the spoils of war. She's *most* pleasing to look at, and her voice?"

"The French call her *'der Engel von La Ciotat'* because her singing is the substance of angels," the shorter one blurted.

Richter, in midstep, paused and swiveled. "An angel, you say?" His hand dropped to the sheath that dangled from his belt. His finger tapped the leather-wrapped handle. "Well then, this angel's wings are about to be clipped."

The metal door flew open and slammed against the stop. "Sit her up!"

Hands grabbed her form and forced it onto a chair in the center of the room.

"Pull off the hood and let me see this *angel* for myself."

With a gleam in his brown eye and glare in his blue, the taller soldier stepped forward and ripped away the burlap sack.

"Hmmm. *Yes.* Most pleasing indeed." The colonel reached into his pocket, grabbed a small bag of coins, and tossed it to the shorter of the two. "Take this for a job well done." His scowl returned to the young girl. "Now, get out!" A shiver of excitement raced along Richter's neck, and a long-suppressed appetite had been stimulated.

I own you.

Friedrich Richter flicked his tongue against dry lips and smiled greedily.

*****

The burlap sack was ripped from her head, but the room didn't come into focus instantly. It was dim, and the air smelled of antiseptic. When her eyes adjusted, a dark form materialized under a cone of white light. A uniform. A Nazi uniform.

He hovered over her.

With every movement, this officer maintained an air of possession. It was as if he inspected a piece of meat at the butcher's shop. Perched on top of a neck squeezed by a high buttoned collar, a ruddy face filled with crooked teeth leered at her. Fingers clamored to his collar and twisted the first button.

Caro wiggled her wrists and ankles, but pieces of rope bit into her flesh. The knots were so tight, she couldn't move. Her limbs were lifeless.

The officer slid a knife from the sheath on his belt and strode behind Caro, out of sight. "*Kleines...*" Caro's eyes darted left and right but could see nothing.

"*Sprichst du Deutsch?*"

A cold blade pressed against her right cheek, and chills sparked along her spine. Her breath caught.

"*Ich bin Oberst Friedrich Richter.*" He leaned an inch from her ear and whispered. His breath was stale and reeked of cigarettes. "*Vielleicht bring ich es dir bei.*" An arm extended around her shoulder, and the blade's point dipped to the top button of her dress. It flicked effortlessly through thread fastening.

A button clinked to the floor, bounced, and stilled.

Mortified, Caro prepared for the worst, *whatever* that could be.

Footfalls echoed to her right, and she caught sight of his dark uniform striding next to her. He crouched on both knees directly in front and pointed the knife at her chest. Cold steel lowered below the hem of her dress and pressed just above her knee. The officer licked his lips and watched the point of the blade slide onto her kneecap, too light to cut but firm enough to send a message.

His thin lips parted, and a chuckle burst forth as if some casual joke had been told.

A devil's laugh! Anger surged in Caro's body and, before even she realized, she spat in his face.

He hit her hard.

Blood filled her mouth and, despite efforts not to, a small whimper escaped Caro's lips.

His mouth twisted in pleasure as he wiped his face with a sleeve. Then his lips peeled back, and clawlike teeth seemed to snarl. He leaned in, a hot breath from her ear. He raised the knife in a deliberate, taunting motion until steel met her throat and scraped along her jugular.

I dare not move.

The blade scraped downward to the silver locket and paused.

Caro's brain reminded her body, *You need to breathe!* She exhaled slowly.

With his free hand, the colonel grasped the chain from the back of her neck and pulled taut against her throat.

Caro struggled against the pressure. Her throat convulsed, and she felt a trickle of blood dribble down her chin.

A vicious chuckle escaped his lips as he lowered them inches from hers. His pencil-thin mustache quaked with pleasure as he released the chain and she gasped for air.

He was smiling in a way that made her skin crawl. The blade slipped to the next button of her dress. Again, a simple flick, and another bounced on the floor. "*Verstehst du nicht?*" The bust of the dress sagged between her breasts. "*Du bist meins!*"

Caro's mind raced. *How am I to fight back?* Fingers tried to clench into fists. But a cool numbness washed through bound, powerless wrists. *I can do nothing.* For the first time since her capture, doubt sprang into her mind.

I'm going to die here.

The German stood tall and removed his field jacket. He tossed it onto the cot and moved behind her again. A warm tongue licked her earlobe. "*Du bist nur meins.*"

Tears welled in Caro's eyes as his two hands reached around her shoulders, cupped her breasts, and squeezed.

I am powerless.

Once more, the flat, cold blade pressed against her cheek and slid down her throat to the last button of her blue summer dress.

Caro sucked in a breath of stale air, closed her eyes, and summoned a scream.

Without warning, the door pounded from outside. The man sighed and straightened. The blade fell to his side. He strode to the door and stepped from the room.

Caro's teary eyes flashed open and searched. Behind her, a curtained partitioning. To her left, a ceramic sink hung on the wall. On her right, the cot upon which she had been dropped when first carried into the room. A sterile tang of antiseptic hung in the air. *Am I in a medical center?* As the door creaked opened and voices grew stronger, she dropped her head. This time, two sets of footsteps echoed closer.

Though squinting, Caro observed a pair of immaculate boots striding toward her.

She tilted her chin slightly to the taller soldier and noticed a small scar on the left side of his forehead just above his eye. This officer wore a smartly tailored uniform. Close-cropped blond hair with white blotches protruded beneath a peaked officer's cap. The officer stared, and, for an instant, Caro recognized something in his face. But it remained unflinching. The two officers mumbled in German until the one with immaculate boots turned to her. His French was flawless.

"The colonel would like to know your name."

She wiggled a little, fighting through the pain as she attempted to separate her mind from the room she sat. Caro's thoughts tried to transport her to a different place. No matter what her captors said, what they asked, she would not respond.

I am no longer in this room.

Richter mumbled a few words in German.

"The colonel says you are 'Daughter of the Maquis.'"

Caro sat mute but followed the officer's gaze to the floor and to the liberated buttons lying at her feet. She glanced up, her eyes steady on his. Did she see pity in his expression? Perhaps he noticed her tear-streaked cheeks, the blood on her chin and would offer some degree of empathy.

He turned to his left toward Richter's field jacket on the cot. "Do you have a name?"

Caro said nothing.

"Perhaps..." The officer nodded. "I should call you, *Caroline*?"

Her body went very still. She tried not to look stunned.

"Daughter of Charles and Anne?" The officer turned to Richter and nodded. "Let me introduce myself, for it has been some time. *Mademoiselle,* I am Lieutenant Hanz Lambrecht. You have already met Colonel Richter."

Caro's fear flew to rage. A guttural, animalistic sound rose like a growl, escaping her lips. "*You!*"

Her mind raced to vague images of immaculate black boots, a teddy bear, a leather case, and lying in the straw loft of her father's boathouse. "*You!* You killed my parents!" An electric prickle shot down her arms and up the back of her neck.

"That was most regrettable but no. I had no part in that."

"Of course, you did! It was *you!*"

"Caro, this is war. Your parents were Maquis. The order came from high command. The only thing I *could* do—"

"Was execute my parents!"

"No, Caro, the only thing I could do was protect you."

"Protect *me*?" Her eyes gaped wide in complete astonishment. "What do you mean *protect* me?"

"Caro, that night, I knew where you were."

"I don't—"

"I knew you were hiding in the boathouse, like your brother, years before."

Caro's mind raced in confusion. "But how? *How* did you know?"

"It's my job to know. My orders that night were to eliminate all threats." Though almost imperceptible, Lambrecht's façade of stone cracked. "I know there are many horrors in war, but none of them should involve children. Through the years, I have done my best to protect as many as possible." A rueful grin cut across his face.

"And *that* makes it okay?"

"It excuses nothing," he said flatly.

Richter rambled in German. After sufficing the colonel, Lambrecht turned to her. "Caro, the colonel requests you to sing for him."

Stunned from Lambrecht's revelation, Caro shook her head in disbelief.

"Apparently, the colonel has heard your voice is the 'substance of angels.' That also was not my doing."

Her head sagged and chest began to heave. "I... I don't believe you." Tears streamed down her cheeks.

"Caro, I can no longer protect you. There is no boathouse for me to hide you in. I urge you to sing."

As sobs rippled into her shoulders, her head slumped forward. And then, something strange snapped deep inside her. She lifted her chin and stared at the officers, a jolt of defiance sprang in her spirit, a newfound confidence expressed in a single word.

"Never."

Richter's tongue wet his lips. He leaned forward, sharpness in his tone. "*Wird die kleine Schlampe singen oder nicht?*"

Strangely, the burning hatred in Caro's limbs dissipated. She eased into a calm bearing, and she muttered, again, quietly and without emotion. "*Never*."

Her imagination slipped from the room, surrounding walls, and building in which she sat. As Caro's mind separated from body, she traveled to a place no one could hurt her.

A small girl ran through a lush green meadow. Tall grasses brushed against her tanned skin. Warmth of the sun caressed her cheeks and arms. A cardboard box dangled in her tiny hands.

"Caro!" Arthur called behind her.

But she giggled and continued running until she approached the meadow's edge. Again, Arthur called after her. Her little legs finally stopped, and she peered into the box.

"I said *wait*! Wait for me!" He ran to her side, out of breath. "We release them together."

Caro nodded, her short raven hair blowing carelessly in the wind.

Each child reached inside and delicately cupped a *cigale*. When arms withdrew from the box, small hands opened. A cicada, perched contentedly on each of their palms, whined a high-pitched reverberation.

"They *sing*!" Caro squealed. She turned to her brother; a smile stretched across his face. "They sing for us, Arthur!"

The insects' wings flickered to life and took to air. Brother and sister watched as both cicadas flew into sunlight and disappeared above the green treetops.

They cannot hurt me anymore.

A peacefulness unlike any she had ever known spread throughout her body.

I am free

EIGHTEEN
Lyon

When the breeze swept through and caressed golden treetops, a myriad of leaves twitched to life. Below, columns of Americans stood dizzy from late-afternoon heat. Weary from hours of marching, the ranks welcomed a breath of coolness and momentary respite. Frank rolled his shoulders, heavy with the weight of a slung rifle and backpack. It was a failed attempt to ease discomfort from an aching back.

Frank tilted his head skyward and sucked in a gulp of fresh fall air. An exaltation of Calandra larks swooped over the treetops, etched against a slate-colored sky. He considered the fact that tree leaves in Europe changed to only hues of yellow in fall. Back home, he'd be quail hunting this time of year. Father on one side, Michael on the other, walking fields of tall brown grass, surrounded by leaves of all colors.

Frank wound his way through a maze of soldiers and neared his unit. He studied the faces he passed. Each man pressed with his own worries. But for him, there was only one true concern, and it had nothing to do with his own life or returning home. Once again, he forced her name to the back of his mind. His eyes scanned the heavens, but his thoughts weighted an aching body firmly to the ground. Suddenly, it was as if his pack was stuffed with all the world's misery and sadness.

The huddling soldiers parted for their sergeant. "Hey, Sarge..." Risaliti gulped from a canteen and wiped lips with a dirty sleeve. "What's next?"

Frank's helmet fell into an open hand as he gathered his thoughts. "Our unit is among several being sent ahead to scout enemy position and resistance. Intel says there are twenty-eight bridges scattered around the city's edge. We need to secure one called Ponts de la Mulatière. Arthur will be our tour guide and get us there." Frank ran his fingers through curls of hair and plopped the helmet back onto his head. "We move out in ten minutes. Arthur..." Frank nudged the French commando. "Follow me."

Separating from the others, the pair walked to the crest of a hill. Below, a flowing Rhône cleaved a sprawling Lyon in half. "What can you tell me about it?" Frank asked.

"Lyon is a big city. Early in the war, it was center for German forces but also a stronghold for French Resistance. Some call it the 'capital of French Resistance.'"

"Why the capital?"

"The Gestapo has had many difficulties here. Hundreds of years ago, *des traboules* were built within city walls."

"*Traboules*?" Frank asked, his eyebrow raised.

"Secret passages built through houses and buildings. Mostly in the old part of the city."

Frank crossed his arms and studied the distant city. "Like above-ground tunnels? Interesting."

"*Oui*."

"How well do you know these passages?"

"I know many lead from the river to places of business. In old times, they allowed workmen and craftsmen to transport clothes and textiles through the city while remaining sheltered from bad weather. Today, they enable Maquis to escape Gestapo raids and move quickly, without being seen. To someone visiting the city, they can be very difficult to find. I had a cousin who lived in Lyon. I visited him several times a year and saw passages firsthand."

"Arthur..." Frank's eyes widened. "Intel suspects German headquarters are in some hospital, a St. Joseph's?"

"I'm familiar with that hospital."

Frank instinctively reached into his shirt pocket, squinting as if in deep contemplation. Fingers opened, and dried white rose petals lay scattered on his palm. "Once this bridge is secured, we'll have a window. A small one, but one where we can do a little of our own reconnaissance."

Arthur nodded. "We find Caro." The Frenchman glanced at the broken bloom in his friend's hand.

"Or die trying." Frank pinched one of the petals and rolled it between his thumb and forefinger.

"Thank you, my friend, for everything," Arthur said.

"Arthur..." Frank cleared his throat and slid the petals back into his pocket. "Your sister. She means quite a bit to me. Perhaps more than—"

"Frank, don't worry. We'll find her."

Frank glanced back at his unit and beckoned. "Let's move out."

Above the line of soldiers, the setting sun cracked through dark cloud cover and walked across the heart of a glowing Lyon.

*****

Equine communication while riding on Grandfather's farm in Kansas was never Michael's strong suit. Frank had always been the superior rider. But here he was, an English-speaking American, sitting upon a French horse.

I wonder if my horse needs a translator?

But the animal's smooth gait seemed equal and balanced. Apparently, over the course of the last couple of hours, he had been doing something right. With each passing mile, falling from his mount and breaking his neck seemed more unlikely.

For a moment, he imagined the war over and being back on his farm in Kansas. Riding this horse reminded him of a normalcy, a comfortability long forgotten. His head tilted back, and he smiled at the stars. There was a peacefulness to riding he couldn't explain. Michael leaned forward in the saddle and let his body follow the horse's motion. His mount pulled even with Maurice's.

Just below the Frenchman's beret, moonlit spirals of his dark hair jumped, keeping time with the action of his trotting horse. The small birthmark on his cheek glistened against his milky-wan complexion and the faint moonlight.

"So, what's the plan?" Michael asked.

"We are traveling to a seminary. We'll be meeting Father Delacroix. He's been there for years. From there, fresh mounts and a direct line to Lyon." Maurice reached into his pack, twisted the lid from a canteen, and swallowed. "Drink?"

"Yes, thank you." Michael reached across and grabbed the canteen. Though his horse's gait seemed smooth, water splashed into his mouth and trickled down his chin.

"We travel by horse because cars attract too much attention," Maurice said. "Even riding a bike without a working rear light can be perilous. Get stopped by Vichy, they check the number of your identification papers, find it doesn't exist? One minute it's riding a bike, the next a chain of inquiries. Finally, you're standing before a firing squad."

"Yeah, that's not good." He returned the canteen. "How many are you in this area, the resistance?"

"In this locale? *Eight*...counting you." Maurice chuckled. "But a friend of mine says, 'The Maquis are as numerous as prostitutes in Paris.' Though I'm pretty sure we get more action."

As their horses glided over the terrain, a three-quarter moon hovered in the black sky. Michael balanced his weight equally on both sides of the horse, but the inside of his legs ached from constant pressure needed to maintain direction. "How much longer before the seminary?"

"Not much." Maurice nodded into darkness. "We're here."

Out of thin air, a small steeple climbed into the night sky, and a silhouette of a crucifix mounted on its top became visible. Pulling the reins, Maurice slowed his horse, and Michael did the same. A whitewashed stone wall encircled the seminary, and the Frenchman dismounted at its front gate.

"Father Delacroix should be waiting," Maurice said. He rapped on a solid wooden gate, and, within minutes, heavy footfalls sounded on the other side.

"I'm coming, I'm coming," a gruff voice barked. A metal latch flipped, and the door parted, screaming on rusted iron hinges. Shrouded in a robe of white, a burly form materialized.

"Father!" With open arms, Maurice embraced the priest, who returned a bear hug. "Good to see you, my friend."

"Good to be seen these days," Father Delacroix quipped, "and not viewed." His thick neck dropped into thicker shoulders that sank into a chest and midsection all of the same width.

This man's form provides no tapering of waist. He's like one large block, robed in white!

Maurice's arm reached toward Michael. "This is Michael, an American friend in need of assistance."

"Michael." The priest extended a massive hand. "May the peace of God be with you."

"And with you, Father." The priest's viselike grip caught Michael by surprise.

"Let's get out of this cold night air. My back is stiff enough," Delacroix said bitterly.

Maurice and Michael led their horses through the gateway. Father Delacroix turned and pushed the heavy wooden doors closed. Iron hinges groaned in protest as the metal latch fell tight. “This old man needs his fire and pipe.” He scurried in the direction of a quaint building sitting beneath the steeple.

As his massive, cloaked white figure bustled across the middle of the courtyard, Michael swore the burliest apparition in existence floated before him. In the middle of the small quad, a large white line appeared below the American’s feet then another crossing it. It looked as if someone had painted markings onto the surface of the ground.

With the horses tied up in the stable, the three men walked through an arched entrance and into small living quarters. An eager fire licked at the last of a log. Hot embers glowed orange red and cast dancing shadows onto the wooden floor.

“Hungry?” The priest grabbed an iron poker and stoked the fire. “Thirsty?”

Both visitors shook their heads.

“Then, sit. Relax. Warm yourselves. You must catch your breath before the final storm.”

Michael and Maurice plopped into chairs already gathered around the fireplace. The men welcomed the radiating heat as a solitary flame crackled to life.

Father Delacroix shuffled to his wooden rocking chair, grunted, and fell into it, rubbing his back. Fishing a pipe out of his pocket, he stuffed the chamber with fresh tobacco. “There were three other priests in this place before the war.” Thick but nimble fingers struck a match and lit the tobacco. As he breathed in, the pipe hissed to life and golden embers radiated in the chamber. “One was killed by a land mine. Another went into the city to care for wounded.” The priest stared into the smoldering pipe chamber.

Michael leaned forward in his chair. “And the last?”

“I don’t know.” After a long inhale on the bit of his pipe, Delacroix exhaled a plume of smoke. “It’s as if he were never born. He walked out the gate one day and never returned." The rhythm of the priest's rocking chair was as steady as a metronome and created a trancelike effect on Michael. "Maurice, you'll need to be very careful. More than usual. An SS battalion moved into a barracks just across the river, near the city. They make reconnaissance sorties at night, even as far as here. You two must also avoid bridges leading into town. And there is a stricter curfew within city limits as punishment for increases of sabotage."

"We'll use the waterway and avoid bridges." Maurice nodded. "Leave that to me."

Tobacco glowed with each of Father Delacroix's puffs. "The only thing prowling city streets these days are cats...and those who move catlike." The priest's ruddy face twisted into a grin.

"How much farther is the city?" Michael asked.

"For you? Forty-five-minute ride. For me? Much longer. I am not built for riding." The priest's hand snatched a woolen blanket that lay on the ground next to his chair. He whipped it open and covered his husky legs. "Do you believe in God, Michael?"

Surprised at the question, Michael continued to stare at the embers in the fireplace. "I was not the most religious guy in the world, especially before the war. It's amazing how jumping from a plane, or living in a foxhole dug to a cowardly depth, makes you cease being an atheist." "A cowardly depth?" the priest asked.

"It just means you dig as deep as possible, and hopefully, nothing can touch you. But I often wonder..." The American turned his head in thoughtful contemplation. "Where is God in times like these?"

"And maybe"—Father leaned forward in his chair; his body stilled—"God is wondering, 'Where is humanity in times like these?'" The priest chuckled and breathed a single word. "Love." Delacroix puffed at his pipe and continued rocking. “If only our world could love more.”

Michael held his hands to the warmth of the fire. “It seems humanity has much to learn.”

“It’s not difficult. I love people, and people love me.” Father banged his pipe onto the arm of the rocking chair. “Except the Nazis.” Pieces of ash fell to the floor. “I *hate* those guys.”

NINETEEN
On Three!

Arthur took point leading the Americans down a winding cobblestone road and to the city's edge. Though Lyon was another in a string of familiar cities and towns, something seemed different. Frank inhaled deeply and realized. The faint but noticeable smell of shooting or burning that seemed to link almost every previous town the soldiers liberated was missing.

The unit scampered behind the French commando until his arm flew up signaling "all stop." A grove of pine trees provided a final piece of cover.

Frank recalled aerial reconnaissance photographs shown at command. Lyon was a maze of roads, buildings, and structures sitting at the junction of two rivers: the Rhône and Saône. Prevailing darkness made navigation all the more challenging. Ahead, the road disappeared into a canyon of man-made buildings, each stone and brick laid in Medieval or Renaissance architecture.

This city is beautiful, Frank thought. Once again, he followed the Frenchman's lead, and the men wound behind. *And largely unscathed by bombing.*

Arthur stopped so suddenly, Frank almost plowed into his back. Arthur's neck craned behind, and he whispered, "Down this road then left."

As the soldiers crossed the road, Piero chuckled. "Isn't this like the movies? Man, this is just like the movies."

Haubert threw a gnarled cigar stub at him, and it glanced off his shoulder. "Shad-up!"

They approached the second intersection, and Arthur's arm flew into a ninety-degree angle, fist closed. He peered around the corner and pulled his head back quickly. "Bridge just ahead." Once more, the commando peeked around the bend. “All clear.” While crossing the intersection, Frank scanned left and right, up and down. Only deserted streets and buildings surrounded them, but danger lurked in every shadow.

As the bridge came into sight, no sign of life was apparent. The unit pressed against a final building, an enormous palazzo, for cover. Frank’s back leaned against the structure’s cold stone wall. Only fifty yards of open road stood between them and their objective. He nodded and gestured signals at two of his soldiers.

Risaliti moved to the left side of the span, Piero to the right. Both men crouched near the ground and stepped onto the bridge. Rifles raised as the unit prepared to cover both scouts if the need presented itself. As the pair sidled to the interior of the span, both leaned over the edge to study the underside. After twenty seconds of inspection, Risaliti craned over his shoulder and eyed Frank. He shook his head and signaled with one hand. Piero did the same. It meant only one thing. The bridge was already wired for detonation.

Both soldiers withdrew across the bridge and approached their unit. In one decisive rush, they scurried back and huddled with their sergeant, kneeling on the ground. Risaliti lifted his helmet, sweaty fingers swiping at a wide forehead. “They attached zinc-lined boxes to the bridge girders, each containing explosives. The system is designed to detonate all charges at once.”

Piero panted with excitement. “They also p-p-placed additional charges at both ends. Charges are attached to an electric fuse and connected by electrical cables.”

“They run through protective steel pipes to a control circuit located in one of the small buildings on the other side.” Risaliti shifted his weight to the other knee. “That way, they can be manually ignited.”

“We need to find that building and secure it.” Frank bit his lip in concentration. “Once on the other side, we’ll follow the steel piping to the building the detonator’s in and disarm it. Move in pairs. Quickly. Silently. Ten-foot spread. Arthur, Piero, Haubert...right flank.” The sergeant’s finger thrust in that direction. “We’ll take the left. Let’s go.” Every ten feet, a pair of soldiers trailed Frank and Arthur.

One step at a time, the men slithered to the halfway point of the bridge’s deck. A dog barked in a nearby alley. The soldiers dropped and pressed upon the stone walls of the bridge like gargoyles. Frank’s muscles froze against the parapet. When barking stopped, he inched forward, peering into darkness. Adrenaline coursed through his veins.

Ten minutes later, the unit gathered on the far side, though, to Frank, the crossing seemed to take ten hours. Arthur pointed to the steel piping winding to a small cottage one hundred yards from their position, a safe distance for detonation. Frank signaled for the men to continue flanking the structure.

One by one, the men shifted into position and knelt along the base of the cottage. Above their heads, a window balanced in the middle of the wall. Sloth-like, Moore stood and peered through the glass. His index finger rose, indicating one sentry. Moore held his position at the window and prepared his rifle, while the others bent around the corner and sandwiched the door. Frank mouthed the countdown and threw out his fingers.

Three...two...one.

In a single motion, Haubert kicked the door open, and soldiers burst into the room, weapons drawn. A lone German soldier sat at a table, leaning over a plate of steaming food. His young eyes widened as if the *Führer* himself had jumped into the room.

Haubert pressed the barrel of his rifle to the private's temple. "*Keine Bewegung!*" A fork in one hand and napkin in the other, the German's hands crawled into the air.

Moore closed the door.

"Riz, to the window. Piero, door. Everyone alert and eagle-eyed." Frank turned and faced their prisoner. "Tell him again, Private Haubert, not to move."

Again, Haubert barked the command in German.

"Hey, Hobs, I hope your German is better than your English." The corners of Risaliti's mouth twisted into a smirk. "For all we know, your West Virginian accent could be asking Fritz here to do the waltz."

Frank moved to the window and peered over Risaliti's shoulder. "Moore, get on the radio. I want engineers up here *now*. I want those explosives unarmed and this bridge secured."

Hands above his head, the German eyed the Americans and forced a smile. "*Ich will Ihnen etwas zeigen—*"

"What the hell's he saying?" Piero asked.

For the first time, Frank considered just how young this soldier looked. "I don't care. Tell him to shut up. *Now!*"

"*Halt die Klappe!*" Haubert snapped at the prisoner. "*Schnautze hab ich gesogt!*"

Frank nudged Moore on the shoulder. "We good?"

"Yeah, engineers on the way. Be here in ten. Tanks and artillery right behind." Moore dropped the handset onto its carriage.

The young German's right hand lowered and set his fork onto the tabletop. "*Ich will Ihnen etwas zeigen—*"

"What the *hell's* he doing?" Piero shouted.

"*Keine Bewegung!*" Haubert commanded.

Reaching into the left side of his overcoat, the German glanced up at the Americans, smiling. "*Bitte, ich möchete Ihnen nur etwas zeigen—*"

"He's going for a gun!" Moore's hand plunged to his sidearm.

"*Keine Bewegung! Keine Bewegung—Stop!*"

But the German's hand continued and slid inside his coat pocket. In a blur, Moore whipped his M1911 pistol from its hip holster. Two gunshots shattered the air and jolted the senses of everyone inside. A deafening concussion reverberated, and the smell of gunpowder infused the tiny room.

The young German's head slumped backward. His body rolled from the chair and crumpled onto the floor.

"What the *hell* was he thinking?" Piero yelled. "What the hell was he doing?"

"Don't know..." Moore's eyebrows flared into his forehead. "But that's one less problem to deal with."

Piero knelt beside him and rolled him over. His face was pale already. Blood streamed from his nostrils.

His eyes fluttered open, and he gurgled a breath. "*Sag es meiner familie...*" The soldiers saw his chest stop rising and the life leave his body. He exhaled and stilled.

Piero reached into his overcoat.

"What is it? A gun?" Risaliti's lips pressed together. "I *knew* it. He was going for a gun."

Piero's face blanked. "Photographs." His hand pulled four black-and-white photographs from the German's coat pocket. "He was reaching for photographs." He flipped through each one. "It was his family. He wanted to show us pictures of...his family."

Frank bowed his head, disgusted at more senseless death. "Haubert, Risaliti, I want a quarter-mile sweep of the perimeter. I need to know if those gunshots were heard." Both men bolted out the door and disappeared into darkness. "Move that body to the back of the room. Cover it."

"W-w-what should I cover him with?" Piero's voice cracked as he stared at the face of the dead German. It was a face no younger than his.

Frank's jaw set in a grim line. "Use his overcoat."

Piero raised the pictures for everyone to see. "What should I do with the photogr—?"

"I don't *care* what you do with them!" Frank snapped. "Put them back! Get rid of them!" Yet, to see a dead enemy this close, to recognize more death, more lost youth, tore at Frank's heart. He buried those feelings behind a war-hardened poker face. "We've got a job to finish—now, get rid of them and focus."

Within minutes, a team of engineers swarmed the bridge, disarming and dismantling the explosives. The door flew open, and Haubert and Risaliti scampered into the room. They huddled around Frank. "Still all clear, Sarge. Nothing."

"We caught a break." Frank heaved a sigh and glanced at Arthur. "Gentlemen, our job here's done, but you know there's something else. Arthur's sister is still out there. And we believe we know where she may be, but the truth is we're not sure." Frank turned in a slow circle, eyeing each of his men. "Now, I'm not asking you to follow me. I just know Arthur needs us." He felt a lump in his throat. "And so does...*Caro*."

"Intel puts German headquarters in the middle of town, a couple of miles from our current position. That's where they would have taken her. For interrogation," Arthur said.

"We already know the Krauts are retreating north. When our tanks and everyone else starts crossing these bridges, it won't be long before they turn tail and run. Any chance of finding her will be gone. We need to get to that hospital before everyone else." Frank's voice lowered in tone. “If you want no part of this, I understand. Stay here. We’ll meet up before morning. If you want to—”

“Sarge...” Moore stepped forward. “I know I speak for everyone. Arthur’s like a brother, and *you?* Well, you’re like a brother, too, but much older.” Hushed laughter echoed in the cramped room. “We’re with you. We’re with you *both*.”

“House to h-h-house, ruin to ruin if that’s what it takes.” Piero set his jaw, and all the men nodded in agreement. “To the end.”

His face alight with hope, Arthur stepped forward. “My friends, my brothers, *merci*. We go, together.”

“Rescuing a damsel in distress? This *is* the s-s-stuff heroes are made of.” Piero opened the door. “I told you this was like the movies.”

“Heroes are drunks.” Moore, flinty-eyed, leaned forward and trailed outside. “Or idiots.”

One by one, the men filed past Frank. He checked the room one final time and glanced at the dead German in the corner. Thick red blood pooled on the ground near the covered body and around four scattered black-and-white photographs.

Visions of broken sunflowers on a cold floor, his own hands covered with a sickeningly sweet odor, snapped inside Frank’s mind. As he closed the door behind and jogged to his men, the mechanical squeaking of metal tracks crescendoed behind the bridge.

Hang on, Caro. I’m coming.

TWENTY
Fresh Mount

An odor of fresh earth hung in the air as the men walked across the cemetery. Michael breathed it in and scanned the area. Everywhere he looked, piles of dirt hunchbacked on the ground. It was as if someone without a map dug for buried treasure with little success.

A terrible thought struck Michael. *Empty pits awaiting bodies and burial.* "My God," he said grimly, "these are freshly dug graves."

"I dug them all day yesterday. In fact..." Delacroix chuckled, "that's all I do anymore. I dig graves." The priest's words trailed into husky laughter emanating from deep inside his barrel-like chest.

"I didn't realize you had so many dead to bury." *Why is a priest laughing about digging so many graves?* Michael gawked, wide-eyed, as he counted over twenty mounds.

"Follow me, my son." Once again, the burly apparition floated across the interior of the quad and toward a small building separated from the others. The priest balanced a thin taper between his thick fingers, casting a glimmer of light onto a faint trail. Twenty yards ahead, a bleached, whitewashed building appeared, terracotta roof tiles capping it. A key ring jingled to life as the priest pulled it from his pocket. "This is the chapel." Father fumbled through his keys, picked one, and thrust it into the keyhole. The wooden door creaked open, and the men entered. Candlelight cast into the room.

Michael's eyes went wide. "Coffins. *Everywhere.* This room is packed with coffins." He shook his head in confusion. "I...don't understand."

Father Delacroix lowered the candle next to one of the closed containers. "Sometimes it's difficult to understand the ways of our Lord." His thick hand grabbed the lid's edge and flipped it open. "Take a look for yourself."

Michael hesitated then stepped forward and peered into the container. His mouth gaped open as he counted an arsenal of handguns and rifles. His voice filled with amazement. "These were..." And then he put the pieces together. "Air dropped? By the Allies!"

"God provides in mysterious ways. Sometimes weapons, sometimes equipment or food." Delacroix lowered the lid and walked between several more canisters and spun around. "The seminary, with its white walls and buildings, makes the perfect drop zone, especially under moonlight."

Frank remembered the painted white lines on the ground. "Outside, in the yard? That's what the X is for? Isn't it? In the middle of the courtyard?"

Delacroix nodded. "X is supposed to mark the spot, but not every drop hits the mark. I've had to repair the steeple three times in the past six months alone." He flipped the lid closed and patted the container top. "My job is to dispose of the containers so Germans never find them. And since they're about the size of coffins? Well, it seems the decent thing to do is give them a proper burial."

Maurice chuckled. "Father's the most popular priest in the province for confession."

"And the most fit." Delacroix arched his back and rubbed his shoulder. "Father also suffers a bad back from all that *damn* digging."

"It is said"—Maurice smiled genially—"'One leaves Father Delacroix's confessional armed to sin.'"

Delacroix leaned on the doorknob. "It is also said, 'All hard work brings a profit. Mere talk, only poverty.' And, if nothing else, it helps pass my day." The priest shuffled through the exit and locked the door behind. "It's nice to dig graves that actually stay empty." He nodded into darkness. "Follow, please. On to the stable."

As the men neared a wooden stable, a scent of straw and animal mixed in the air. Once again, visions of Grandfather's farm struck Michael.

Father Delacroix stepped to the farthest stall. "Michael, you get to ride Claire. She's my favorite."

Candlelight flickered into the stall and Michael stared in disbelief. "I thought you said these were *fresh* mounts?"

"These are fresh mounts." A smile spread on the priest's face.

Maurice reached into another stall and pulled a bicycle out. "Don't you know how to ride?"

"Of course, I just thought..." Michael snorted in surprise.

"From here, bicycles are much quieter and easier to hide," Maurice said. "Terrain is relatively flat from here to the city. I know the trails quite well." Both men walked their bicycles to the front gate.

Delacroix flipped the latch and pushed the gates open. "Remember," he said, spinning around, "the path of righteousness is often a dangerous one."

Michael extended a hand. "Thank you, Father. I'm forever in your debt."

But the priest pulled him into a tight bear hug. "*Michael...*God helps those who help themselves. Now, go in peace, my friends." Delacroix sighed. "Until you see Germans."

*****

A line of soldiers wound through the streets, moving in short bursts. A series of quick, hustling sprints interspersed with pauses of uncertainty. For every moment of question, Frank held one belief with conviction. Each step brought him closer to Caro.

In the distance, a small explosion echoed over the rooftops. Though darkness blanketed the city, inside every window, on top of every rooftop, or in the crack of a doorway, a potential sniper could lay in waiting for the slightest opportunity. It seemed to Frank, revolving eyes darted in all directions. As his soldiers zigged then zagged, human figures dissolved into doorways and melted behind curtains.

This city is a labyrinth.

Banks, hotels, restaurants, apartments, and many other buildings walled them inside these man-made canyons. And while intense bombing reduced other cities to dust and rubble, Lyon seemed mostly unscathed, passed over by war's fickle finger of fate. But for a city of almost seven hundred thousand people, the streets were largely deserted.

Onward the men advanced.

"This damn city's a maze!" Haubert pulled a mangled cigar out of his mouth, hawked, and spat on the ground.

"Good thing we've got Arthur," Moore chirped. "Otherwise, we'd be as lost as Riz in a brothel."

Small-arms fire and an explosion rattled in the distance. Around the next corner, Arthur slowed the line. Three men in civilian clothing gathered there under an unlit streetlight. They wore the familiar Basque berets of the Maquis.

"Let me talk to them." Arthur approached the men and uttered a few words of indiscernible French. Nodding, he continued the conversation while everyone else waited, then jogged back. "They say some Germans *are* holed up in the hospital. Many bridges destroyed, or being destroyed. We were very lucky to cross. German resistance overall is light and scattered as most retreat out of the city and head north toward Dijon."

Frank's face, cut with hard lines, softened. "Are we close to the hospital?"

"Almost. It's near the Rhône. We'll continue through the heart of the city then cut over. Let's go." Arthur spun and moved fast.

Once again, the line wove around buildings and through thoroughfares. After fifteen minutes of humping it, a mammoth spire perched in front of the soldiers. Despite the darkness, its sharp vertical roofline climbed the night sky and dwarfed the men.

"That's it," Arthur said, slowing to a stop. "Straight ahead."

The tower split the hospital at its midpoint and rose over three-hundred feet above the rooftops of its two wings.

"Damn place is *big*," Risaliti said. "Don't look like a hospital. Looks more like a hotel. What's the plan?"

"I was told German headquarters occupies a small part of the building." Arthur licked his lips. "There're still patients inside, and it's believed they're on the west side of building." He unscrewed the top of his canteen and swigged.

"Let's continue along this road. Move fast. Move smart. Eyes alert," Frank commanded. "West, to the hospital."

Piero advanced to the point and loped across the street as the others trailed behind.

Moore chased after him. "Aren't *you* the brave one?"

"Honestly, my b-b-bravery only improves when others are w-w-watching." Piero chuckled.

PKOW!

The air splintered with a single gunshot. Reflexively, every man dove behind the nearest cover.

"What the *hell* was that?" Risaliti screamed.

"Sniper. Flash in tower of the hospital," Moore deadpanned.

"*Damn!* That was close. Too close." Piero peeked around the tree he hid behind. "You s-s-sure they're up there?"

"That's where I'd be. And if there's snipers in that tower, Sarge, we're going to have to double back."

"I *know*." Frank's mood darkened. "This won't work." *Come on, Taylor, think! Unless...Unless...* "Arthur, where'd you say those *traboules* were?"

Arthur squinted. "*Traboules? Traboules!* Of course. Let me think. *Yes!* There's one not far from here. Frank, any statue of a lion's head marks the entrance to a passageway, and I believe there's one in a courtyard due south. Maybe a quarter mile from here. If we take it, we lose little time."

Frank backtracked under the protection of a tree line and approached the commando. "Lead the way."

Arthur peeled back, pressed along a stone wall, and drifted in the direction he had just traveled. The other men slid backward and followed the Frenchman's gait. The soldiers raced down a side street, turned right, and kept the pace. Pressing against the walls of a narrow alley, three rectangular stone benches, no more than a single foot from the narrow road, appeared in the distance. Past the benches, the roadway suddenly widened, and an iron fence encircled a courtyard to their right. In single file, the men funneled through the opened gate and onto the grass.

"There has to be a lion's head somewhere." Arthur spun around, scanning the area. "It'll mark the entrance to the *traboules*."

The men searched each side, corner, and recess of the courtyard.

"Hey, g-g-guys!" Piero stammered with excitement. "I didn't find a head...I found the whole damn lion!"

Beneath two towering poplar trees rising into the air, a life-sized golden lion glistened in the moonlight. The statue perched on a concrete block. Behind the lion, a row of pine trees leaned against a side of the building.

"I'll be damned," Moore muttered.

"I'm predy sure ya already are." Haubert snorted.

Arthur squeezed between the line of trees and looked straight up, studying the pristine façade. Sweeping arches of sandstone dominated the building's side, but any sign of an entrance could not be found. Finally, Arthur's eye caught a diminutive arc rising gracefully three feet from the base of the wall, largely obscured by the drooping pine boughs. "This way!" Arthur scraped through the branches and leaned against a wooden door built more for a hobbit than a human. The hinges groaned against his weight. Arthur pushed the door open, and a pitch-dark corridor revealed itself.

"Use this." Frank handed the commando a flashlight. "Let's move."

Once inside, the men marveled at the architecture. To the surprise of the soldiers, the passage never widened more than four feet but rose eight-and-a-half feet high. Arched stone cross vaults hung overhead as the men filed past green granite monoliths. Every footfall echoed over stone tile below and between vaulted arches above.

Hang on, Caro! Frank forced a breath to calm himself and loosen his grip on the rifle.

Risaliti's voice reverberated from the end of the line. "Hey, guys, when we rescue Caro, and if we're living tomorrow? We gonna party like there's no tomorrow!"

After about 100 yards, Arthur's pace slowed to a jog. "We're almost there." At the terminus of the hallway, another closed door blocked their exit. Arthur leaned against it and pushed, but the solid wooden door didn't budge.

Frank slung his rifle around his shoulder and pressed both hands to the door. His boots dug into the floor. "Together. *Push!*" The bottom edge of the door ground against the tile and screeched. All at once, the door crashed open, and the two soldiers spilled onto a cobblestone street. The others stepped through the exit and gathered against the far wall.

Arthur pointed in the direction he nodded. "Straight across is the hospital."

Frank's eyes scaled the building's height and examined it for any warlike trap. The others bunched around. "We take it slow. Paratroopers do not run to their deaths."

"No," Moore muttered to Haubert. "They fall to them."

"Five-yard spread," Frank commanded. "Across the street, to *that* door."

The men slinked across and leaned flat against a hospital wall. Hidden under the building's shadow, the men shuffled toward the entrance. An explosion echoed in the distance, and the men looked at Frank. "They're demoing bridges. We need to move. *Now.*"

A gust of wind swept through the alley, and Risaliti eyed a rectangular piece of paper dancing across the ground. He bent over and snatched it. Flipping the card over, he read the print. "La Su Tat?"

Moore turned to him. "*What?*"

"It's a postcard of La Su Tat," Risaliti replied. "And who's Aunt Sissel?"

Moore's hand shot out and snatched the card. "It's not 'La Su Tat,' you idiot. It's *La Ciotat*! How many times I have ta tell ya?"

Frank's mouth dropped open, and he spun around. "*What'd* you say?"

Moore handed him the postcard. “Riz found this against the wall over there, on the ground.”

Frank reached into his pocket and pulled another card out, the one from Caro’s kitchen. He held both side by side.

“Would ya look at that?” Haubert exclaimed. “Dem match!”

“Arthur!” Frank shouted. “Look at this!”

Arthur’s eyes widened. “Frank, she’s been here! She’s alive!”

Electric urgency throttled Frank’s senses. “My God...*Caro’s alive!*”

TWENTY-ONE
All Is Blue

Richter stood behind the chair, out of Caro's sight. Chuckling. Without warning, his hand slammed against her forehead and yanked her head backward until it cracked against the chair top, pinning it in place. Her neck strained against his pull.

Caro felt a vulnerability open up inside of her and expand, threatening to suffocate her. *This is the end,* she thought. Tears stung her eyes and all she saw were teeth, horribly crooked teeth.

Breath, hot and heavy, rolled onto her face.

Caro struggled to move her bound wrists, but they were thick and dull. *That laugh!* All sensation in her arms had deserted her long ago.

Hope deserted her as well.

I'm defenseless! With the back of her head pressed against his chest, he waved a silver dagger in front of her. It dangled inches from her face like a conductor's baton keeping time for an orchestra of demons. Light glittered off the blade's side into her eyes. *Those horrible teeth!*

Arthur, my brother... The steel point pressed against her jugular. *Frank! I'm so sorry. So sor—*

With a sudden rip, the blade sliced deep through her delicate skin. A warm sensation engulfed her neck, her chest, and washed onto her lap. Caro tried her best to blink the sleepy feeling away. Though her mind remained surprisingly lucid, it seemed to wander from her body. She hovered above the room. *I can see...*

No pain. No fear. Only numbness then a lush, verdant meadow under a majestic blue sky.

I can see only...

It engulfed. It welcomed.

Blue...everything is blue.

Tall grass appeared, and she ran through, feeling it brush against tanned skin. Another child, behind her, shouted in laughter. Caro's gaze shot upward, into the dazzling blue light. Warmth from the sun caressed her face and arms. And, just above, a *cigale* flew, out of reach. She continued to chase. Its reverberating wings clicked a familiar song. *I'm so tired, so tired...so tired.*

When her eyes grew much too heavy, she closed them, and only one thought remained.

All is blue.

A pair of bicycles maneuvered through darkness. Michael glanced at the three-quarter moon, thankful for at least a sliver of light to illuminate the terrain. "I thought you said there was a trail?" Michael's legs pumped to keep up with the Frenchman.

"There is." Maurice swerved to the right. "Watch that hole."

But Michael reacted too late, and his tire sank. The hit jarred his back, and familiar pain shot throughout his body. Ignoring the discomfort, he pedaled harder.

"We're almost there." As Maurice reached the apex of the next hill, he slowed then slid to a stop. Michael drew even and skidded next to him. The Frenchman nodded at the valley before them. "Lyon." Even against a black sky, the vastness of this city stretching before them was obvious. Building after building snuggled close to two rivers shimmering under moonlight. Small fires ringed the city's edge. "Bridges are being detonated by Germans to slow the Americans," Maurice said.

"How do we get into the city?"

"A boat. And then some friends." Maurice chuckled. "It's not Paris, but our Maquis brothers and sisters have been quite busy. Let's go."

Tires spun to life as they glided down the hill and into the city environs. Michael pedaled hard and followed the Frenchman's bike. Near the river's edge, an odor of conflagration entered his nostrils, and the pace slowed.

"This way." Maurice veered right then left and decelerated his bike to a silent stop. "From here," he whispered, "we walk."

Both men dismounted their bikes and pushed them along a faint trail. A line of bushes emerged out of the darkness, and Maurice shoved his bike underneath. Michael wheeled his under the row of bushes and turned to find the Frenchman already ten feet away, hiking along the bank. "It's here...somewhere."

"What is?" Michael whispered.

"A large boulder surrounded by six poplars. While Father Delacroix could probably walk across, we'll need a skiff." Maurice disappeared into darkness as the American scanned the riverside.

"*Over here,*" Maurice's voice echoed quietly.

Michael stalked in his direction, and an immense boulder took shape in the blackness. Maurice squeezed between two trees next to the rock and disappeared into the foliage. A shuffling of branches and a grinding sound in the dirt cracked the night air. Maurice reappeared, sliding a small boat toward the water. The wooden hull groaned against dirt and pebbles. "We cross here. Then to safe house. Meet with my friends who'll get us to your friends."

The skiff glided across the debris-filled water. Just a few hundred yards up the river, remnants of a bridge smoldered against the night. A trail of ebon smoke blackened an already-dark sky. The boat's prow nudged into the opposite bank and jerked to a halt. They jumped onto land, lugged the boat into some hedges, and jogged along the riverbank. Maurice scampered over a hill, and before they realized it, walked on a cobblestone road. He pressed against the building sides and moved catlike through a neighborhood of shadows. A modest house, sandwiched between two larger ones, came into view. Maurice rapped on a side door four times.

After a shuffling of footfalls on the other side, a brittle voice responded, "*Qui êtes-vous?*"

"Aunt Maynard is home," he whispered.

The door creaked open, and a dark-haired woman with a thin, ruddy face glared through the crack. "Ahhh, Maurice! Come in, come in."

"*Merci*. Aunt Maynard, this is Michael."

The woman's deep-set dark eyes softened. "Come. Everyone waiting downstairs." Arthur and Michael followed the woman's slender form down a set of stairs. An acrid odor of cigarette smoke wafted across Michael's face. Smoke hung like a cloud in the musty basement. The only light came from an oil lamp flickering against the blacked-out windows. Two men sat at a table cleaning guns.

"This is Pierre and Jaques. They've been with us from the beginning," Aunt Maynard said. Both nodded at Michael. "Operating the radio over in the corner is Felix." Felix sat statue-like at a table. Headphones smothered his ears as he scribbled notes onto a pad. "And over here, we have two newly arrived friends from Southern France. They say they've been chasing Germans for weeks."

Two men sat on a couch in a dark corner whispering. As Michael approached, both stood. The shorter one extended his arm. "Laurent. A pleasure to meet you."

"I'm Michael."

A swirl of blond hair protruded under a black beret of the taller man. "Malory." He stepped forward. "A pleasure to meet you."

Michael grinned and noticed a strange occurrence within this man's face. *His eyes...one is blue, and the other...* "The pleasure's mine."

Brown.

*****

The heavy metal door slammed as footsteps walked in front of her motionless form. Caro felt drugged but aware of noises around her. She was tapped on the shoulder. But her slumped head could not move. Two fingers pressed against her neck, searching for a pulse. "Caro? *Caro?*" Caro's eyelids felt heavy and reluctant at first. But her eyes flicked open, and then an immaculate pair of boots came into focus. "Good morning."

"*Quoi?*" She returned from a long way away and straightened in her chair. "Wwwhat happened?"

"I believe you passed out from exhaustion. After you declined to sing for our dear colonel, there was an explosion nearby, and we were called from the room." Lambrecht stared into Caro's eyes and smiled. "Other than some bruises, a lack of sleep, food, and water, and an undue amount of stress, I believe you'll make a *full* recovery."

Caro stared into Lambrecht's blue eyes, blinking away confusion. "An explosion?"

"In an effort to slow the Americans, Lyon's bridges are being destroyed. Germans are fleeing the city as we speak." The lieutenant pulled a dagger from its sheath and moved behind her. "I wanted to check on you. Make sure you were fine."

Caro heard the blade slice through the ropes binding her hands and legs. With wrists freed, she massaged them in an attempt to wipe away pain and numbness, but her fingers remained thick and clumsy. "When we left you, Richter ordered more snipers to the roof to buy time for our escape." The German officer walked in front of her chair and knelt on one knee. "Are you hungry?" Lambrecht pulled a handkerchief from his overcoat and unwrapped a flaky croissant.

Caro's eyes narrowed, but her hunger gnawed. Still rubbing her wrists, she nodded and grabbed the roll. "Is he?"

"Coming back? No. He scurried away like the rat he is."

"But aren't you going with them?" She nibbled on the bread.

"Yes and no. I do have to leave the city. No self-respecting German officer can be captured in Lyon." The lieutenant winked and tilted his head as if in thought. "Caro, when this war is over, I hope you find your beautiful voice." A look passed between them. For a moment, Caro felt like the little girl waiting for the teddy bear to drop into her small, outstretched hands. "What were those words you sang to me so many years ago?" A broad smile eased across his face, and he stood tall.

Caro stuffed the remaining roll into her mouth and stared at the officer.

"By the light of the moon?" In a whimsical tone, he sang. "*By the light of the moon, I make my escape. By the light of the moon.*" Striding into the doorway, he paused before spinning around and catching Caro's eye. A smile still creased his face. "Simply *magnifique.*"

Caro wiped her mouth with a dirty hand. "The scar, the one above your eye. How did you get it?"

"*This?*" Lambrecht's hand rubbed his forehead. "When I first met my wife, I tripped over my own feet after drinking too much." A chuckle escaped his lips. "I was in love, Caro, and being in love is an intoxication of insanity. Sometimes we say and do things others would declare as nothing more than madness."

She stared at the lieutenant, surprised by his honesty.

"When you're in love, you'd give up everything, even pride. It's the most humbling emotion anyone can experience. Imagine, the need to do anything, sacrifice everything, just for one person. It's most human yet most...*divine*." Lambrecht straightened his back and tugged on his black overcoat. "And now, I long *only* for an end to this miserable war and a return home to my family."

Caro studied the German's eyes and allowed herself a faint smile. "I hope you make it to them. Thank you...for helping me."

"Caro, despite what you may think, there still is kindness in this world. There still is compassion and good and beauty. Remember, child, always to the light." Lambrecht shook his head and grinned. "For when angels like you fly, it is always to the light. And with that, I bid you *adieu*." The officer tipped his peaked cap in her direction, spun, and disappeared out the door.

For a moment, she stared into an empty doorway, unsure what to think.

She pushed against her seat. Unsteady legs trembled beneath her, though they still supported her weight. Severed rope lay at Caro's feet, and she kicked at it with disdain, almost falling over. Edging to the doorway, she recalled the direction and steps her captors had taken upon their arrival. When she reached the stairwell, smoke wafted through the hallway, and a terrible thought struck her.

This building is on fire.

TWENTY-TWO
To the Light

Dank, stale air hung thick. Michael breathed in and welcomed it. For the first time in weeks, tension in his body dissipated as he eased into a chair. Finally, he was on the verge of rejoining his men. Despite a plane crash, multiple searches in the countryside by the enemy, a roomful of German officers only feet from where he stood, and seven shots fired inches from his chest, here he sat.

Michael shook his head, trying to drive out the sleep his body needed. Reaching underneath his shirt, he pulled a silver chain from around his neck then twisted its links. *Albert...Geneviève, I pray you are well.* He kissed the St. Christopher medallion and tucked it under his shirt. His mind drifted to the end of war and a return home.

"Michael?" Maurice strode to the side of Michael's chair. "We leave soon. Reports are coming in. The Germans are pulling out. But, for now, relax."

A sense of relief filtered through Michael's thoughts. The Frenchman turned and walked next to the radioman, Felix. Michael glanced across the basement at the two who cleaned guns. Though he understood little of the French language, the look of two friends sharing a good story was quite familiar. Their faces radiated from some tale of sweet remembrance. *Perhaps a story of better times.* Both chuckled. In the far corner, the two other Maquis sat mumbling.

The letter!

His hand slid into his undershirt, where fabric parted at the lining. This inner seam allowed him to have a "secret compartment," and it had kept the letter intact for the duration of war. Not only did it conceal the paper, it allowed him to always have it close to him. Ironically, it rested just below the same spot Sarah had stolen so long ago, his heart. Unfolding the paper, he stared at the worn parchment and ebony words. He glanced at the date, surprised by the passage of time. She had penned it sixteen months earlier.

Reading the letter comforted Michael and eased his mood. It carried his mind to a better time and a happier place. Once, the page had contained a hint of her perfume, but that had long since disappeared. Yet, every time he read it, he still smelled the lemony scent of her hair, heard her delicate voice, and could feel the softness of her skin. This one piece of paper lifted his spirit higher than the heavens and hardened his resolve to return home. He couldn't imagine any stronger feeling than the force urging him home to his family.

Dear Michael,

I pray this letter finds you well. It seems all my hours these days are filled with prayer, thoughts of you, and of your safe return. Mother and Father are quite well considering both their sons fight a war 4,000 miles away. The time apart from you and your brother has worn their faces and spirits. Though they don't smile as often, nothing can't be cured by both your arrivals.

Coping without you has taken its toll on me as well. Today, I drove into town and walked around the park. Nothing eases a troubled soul like the uncontained, innocent laughter of children at play. After some time at the park, I walked toward the train station. I found myself pretending the war was over and I picking you up. Excitement grew in my heart as I heard a train whistle, and a belching steam engine slowed along the steel rails. I climbed the steps to the platform in haste and, before I knew it, found myself standing there, searching for you. On that platform, at that moment, I thought I would see all I hold dear to me.

My husband. My love. My life.

And as I looked, my heart stopped.

Caskets draped with American flags lined the floor as far as the eye could see. Slowly, I walked by each one, reading the name of the soldier inside. I could do nothing but cry. I probably shouldn't be telling you such sad thoughts, for I want you happy and of sound mind and spirit, but I also know you'd want to hear what troubles me. Please know I wait for you with an anticipation I cannot express with words. I long to lie by your side and stare into the night sky, holding your hand like we first did so many years ago.

I'm going to ask a favor of you. On the next night, you are able, I want you to gaze into the heavens. Find the North Star and smile. When you do, know I, too, look upon that same star. And at that moment, we will be connected. We will be connected in the most heavenly of ways, for all eternity.

While this may not be the happiest of letters, I am too sad to do better, knowing I will never be whole until your return. Please take care of yourself and remember...always look to the light.

All my love,
Sarah

Michael folded the paper, careful not to wrinkle it any more. Letters. They keep a soldier's chin and heart uplifted, even in the darkest of times.

Once more, he slid the letter into the open seam and buttoned his shirt. *I'm so, so tired.* His head jerked to the side as if too much contemplation created a physical burden of melancholy for him to carry. His head slumped against the back of the chair, and his body twitched.

Michael forced himself awake.

In the corner, Maurice whispered to Felix. Turning to the others, a frown arched his lips. "We go now. It seems there's trouble near the hospital." At the table, the men cleaning guns finished. "The Germans have fled Lyon and continue north." Maurice walked to the table and stuffed a revolver into the back of his pants. "Our brothers and sisters need our help. Let's make this right."

He bounded up the stairs, and everyone trailed behind.

Smoke rolled down the open stairwell and coiled around her legs. She clung to the handrail. One step after another, she made sure not to miss a stair. Despite the dimness, her eyes adjusted, and at each level, Caro glanced down the hallway, first one floor then the next. While the smoke did not overpower senses, on the third level it thickened. Moans and wailing pierced the hazy air. Her small feet froze as she scanned the immediate area. Several forms shuffled near the steps.

Patients from the hospital! Some of them hobbled, some stumbled, and others stood dazed.

"Over here!" Caro beckoned the people. "The stairs! They're this way!" In an instant, she leapt from the step on which she stood and streaked through the smoke. Ignoring the pain still ringing around her wrists and ankles, she waved her arms. "The exit's at the bottom of the stairs! Keep going. That way, that way!"

Men and women of all ages brushed by her and disappeared down the stairwell.

An old woman with a bandaged head and an arm in a sling bumped into her, choking on the thickening smoke. "My husband, *please!* My husband's still in his room! I don't have strength to—"

"I'll help him! What's his name?"

"Gabriel."

"I'll get him. Go, down the steps, out the door. *Go*, go now!" Caro spun and charged through the hallway. Dense, pungent smoke wafted between strides and billowed into the ceiling.

"*Gabriel*? Gabriel!" Nothing but darkness enveloped the hallway then a form materialized straight ahead. "Gabriel?"

The man shook his head. "No, no."

"I'm looking for Gabriel! Which room?"

His bony finger pointed across the hallway.

"*Merci*. Keep going. The stairs are straight ahead."

His legs never stopped until he disappeared through the smoke.

Caro raced into the room. A white-haired man lay on the floor, holding his side. He leaned on an elbow and looked up, into her eyes. As she knelt beside him, a weak smile cut across his lips. "Gabriel?"

The old man nodded.

"I'm here to get you out." She slipped a hand under his elbow and helped him stagger to his feet.

Gabriel slung his arm around her shoulders, distributing weight onto her form, and they hobbled through the doorway. "What's your name, daughter?"

"Caro."

"Caro?" They leaned on each other and stumbled to the steps. "I've been rescued. By an angel. And her name is Caro." Gabriel stared into Caro's face and her hair brushed against his cheek. "And a beautiful angel at that."

"Flattery will get you nowhere." Caro's words splintered into spasmodic coughing as she inhaled a gulp of smoke. We need to go—quickly." They limped down from the top stair. "We have two more floors. Together. Use one hand on the rail."

The old man grabbed the handrail while still clinging to Caro's neck. She glanced at the hallway they had just fled. Flames licked walls, and a sound like a furnace inhaling one giant breath rumbled into the stairwell. She glanced at the steps beneath her feet, careful not to lose her balance, and clung to Gabriel's arm. "One at a time. Careful."

"*Merci*, Caro. *Merci*."

TWENTY-THREE

Open Arms

Frank clutched his rifle so hard, his fingers were going numb. "You ready?"

His men leaned forward, their guns drawn, ready to surge through the hospital entrance.

Arthur, his face sculpted like stone, nodded.

"Hey, Sarge..." Risaliti scanned the top of the hospital. "I think it's on fire. *Look*." Smoke poured through one window at least three floors up. Flames leapt from the façade even higher in the structure. Their orange-red hue matched morning light.

Just as Frank stepped forward, the door to the hospital flew open and slammed against the stop. People streamed out. Men on crutches, women in bandages, people of all ages and injury trailed down the steps and spilled into the street.

"They're patients. From the hospital." Moore holstered his sidearm.

A woman seemingly more wide than tall tripped over a crutch supporting her and tumbled onto the cobblestone street, hands first. "Sarge, what'll we do?" Piero yelled.

"Help them!" Frank barked.

Piero slung his rifle around his shoulder, ran to the woman, grabbed the crutches, and pulled her to her feet. Haubert seized the handles of a stretcher from a man who struggled under its weight.

"Arthur and I are going in. You guys, get these people to safety! Stay alert. Looks like the Germans are gone, but ya never know."

Each soldier scrambled to assist someone in need.

Frank turned to Arthur. "Let's go!" Both men slid past the snaking line of patients exiting the building.

"We'll start on the first floor and work our way up. You take the rooms on the right! I'll take the left!"

Both soldiers charged forward swallowed by darkness and smoke.

*****

"One more floor!" Caro winced under the weight of the old man. Bruises and the strain of the last few days depleted her to near exhaustion. One step at a time, they pressed downward.

But Gabriel's shoe slipped on the third step from the top, and he stumbled forward, arms flailing. Caro's hands flew out and snatched the back of his shirt, reeling him back.

The Frenchman clutched the rail in terror then regained his balance. "Thank you, daughter." A coughing spasm shook the old man. "That was close."

Caro wound her right arm around his waist, and they continued.

"One could say...I almost fell...for an angel."

Smoke engulfed them in a cloudy haze. Gabriel leaned hard on the rail, lessening the weight placed on Caro's shoulders, but still, her legs strained to the point of buckling. They stepped onto the final landing, and Caro glanced up the stairwell they had just descended, searching for any falling debris.

"Almost there!" Caro said, breathing heavily.

Gabriel's grip on the railing loosened, and they struggled as one limping form through the doorway. Morning light dazzled their eyes as they staggered clear of the building and into fresh air.

We made it!

An old woman broke from the crowd. "Gabriel! *Gabriel*!" She moved in an awkward gait, her face streaked with tears. "I thought I'd never see you again." His wife wrapped her good arm around her husband's shoulder while the other hung from its sling. Both women supported Gabriel's weight across the street until he collapsed onto a wooden bench.

Mauriel, I'd like you to meet Caro."

"*Merci*, my dear, *merci*." The woman slid onto the bench next to her husband and buried her sobbing head into the old man's chest.

Gabriel clutched his wife. "Caro's my angel. My guardian angel. *Merci,* daughter."

Caro bent down and kissed the old man's cheek. "You're most welcome, Gabriel." She turned, facing the burning building. Though chaos swirled, her bearing eased. The morning sun lit her face, and she absorbed its warmth. Something deep inside her soul sprang to life.

It resounded throughout her being and echoed with every thought.

I'm free.

*****

"Caro? *Caro!*" Frank scanned one room then scurried to the next. "*Arthur!* Anything?"

A voice ripped through hazy air. "No, nothing! And the smoke's getting worse!"

Fumes singed Frank's throat and eyes as he tried to suppress another cough. Keep looking!" The men scurried room to room, but upon reaching the end of the corridor, they were no closer to finding her than when they began.

"Have to move to the second floor!" Arthur yelled. But halfway up the stairwell, smoke veiled their path and overpowered them. Both coughed uncontrollably and struggled with any visibility.

"We need to try the other staircase. *Hurry!*"

Arthur spun, extended his foot, and missed the stair below. He tumbled awkwardly head over heels and he crashed onto the wooden floor with a sickening crunch.

"Arthur!" Frank jumped the remaining steps two at a time and knelt next to his friend.

A low moan emanated from the Frenchman's lips. "My leg..."

Athur's leg bent under his body at an angle no leg should be twisted.

"I can't move it." Arthur grimaced. He pushed off the floor, trying to stand, but collapsed with a scream of agony. "Leave me! *Find* Caro!"

Frank slid his hands under Arthur's armpits and pulled him to his feet. "I've got you. Let's go."

"No! Frank... Get Caro first!"

Together they hobbled down the hallway. Smoke tore at watering eyes, blurring his vision, but within a few minutes, Frank grasped the exit door frame with his free hand and thrust both their bodies through the aperture. They staggered half a dozen steps and collapsed onto the open ground in a heap. Arthur moaned, clutching his leg. Next to him, Frank doubled over on his knees, coughing.

Doctor! We need a... Doctor!" Frank bent, hacking and gasping for breath.

A slim, spectacle-wearing man dressed in a soot-smeared coat scurried toward the men. Kneeling next to the commando's side, he examined Arthur's leg. "Not to state the obvious, but the leg's broken. He'll be fine, but we have to set it. Over there." The doctor pointed to a small palazzo across the street. "A makeshift hospital. We need a stretcher."

Frank caught sight of two of his men. "Haubert! Risaliti! Carry Arthur!" Both soldiers scurried to the commando and scooped him into their arms.

Arthur's eyes locked onto Frank's as they lifted him off the ground. "Find her, Frank!" His voice cracked in pain. "*Find Caro!*"

The doctor patted Frank on the shoulder and stood. "He'll be fine."

Arthur pointed a trembling finger at Frank. "Find her, Frank!" The men disappeared into a crowd of onlookers. Arthur's voice lingered from the street. "*Hurry!*"

Frank turned back to the burning building and peered into a plume of black smoke that hugged the nearby rooftops. His hands rubbed immeasurable weariness from his face as a desperate realization rushed throughout, gripping him in fear. *How?*

Civilians raced every direction, carrying buckets splashing with water and hoses to fight the fire. He scanned the burning hospital, knowing he couldn't even get to the second floor, emotion coursed within him unlike anything he remembered in battle. He was trapped in the eye of some chaotic hurricane.

How am I going to find her? He inhaled deeply, letting fresh air fill his lungs. More than anything in the world, he wanted to hold Caro in his arms one more time. *I have to try.* He gathered himself and prepared to stand.

And then, it came.

"Frank?"

Cradled beneath a bustle of activity, the words carried on the breeze and echoed softly in his ears. At first, his mind ignored what senses tried to interpret, for it was only a sound hidden beneath the chaos swirling around him.

"Frank?"

He scanned the area, concentrating on the crowded street.

A figure surged forward through a storm of people.

"Frank!" Morning light cut through the mist and illuminated her in a golden glow.

He blinked in disbelief. And when his eyes locked onto her raven hair, his heart skipped across the universe. *Caro?* Rising from his knees, all pain and tiredness vanished. He slipped into long strides and threw open his arms. "*Caro!*"

She reached for him, and when their bodies met, Frank folded himself around her and considered never letting go. "Caro, I knew..." Both of them shook with emotion. He leaned back, looked into her tear-streaked face, and lost his breath. "I always knew."

TWENTY-FOUR
A Thousand Years

A vast interior packed with people gave Frank the unmistakable impression he attended a sporting event. At one end of the cavernous hall, a stage rose to a height of five feet and overlooked a dance floor extending nearly the length of a football field. Tables and chairs crammed every available space. On the west interior wall, a balcony hovered over the entire scene and supported so many onlookers, Frank wondered what kept it from collapsing.

Conversation, laughter, and shouting rang throughout the structure. And almost everyone drank champagne. A dozen or more bottles topped most tables, along with copies of the local newspaper, proclaiming the headline *"Lyon Libéré!"* Frank chuckled as soldiers refused to let waitresses remove empty bottles from their tables as they competed to see who could consume the most alcohol.

A mix of cigarette and cigar smoke laced the air and hovered in the wooden rafters overhead. As the thick haze rose, diffused cones of light descended onto the scene, creating a dreamlike atmosphere. But victory over the Germans was no dream. With liberation of Lyon complete, it was time for celebration.

Frank glanced at the stage as trained animals, tumblers, and jugglers ran through their acts. He reminisced of younger years and traveling circuses. American soldiers all around him shrieked their approval.

Holding Caro's hand, Frank snaked through the crowded hall of GIs, leading her to a table.

"Hey, Sarge!" Haubert bellowed. "What kept ya?"

He pulled a chair out for Caro then sat next to her. "We were visiting Arthur."

"How is he?" Piero asked.

"Doctor says he'll be fine." Frank's eyes found Caro. She smiled and leaned into his arm. "Just needs a few more weeks to mend."

Moore's eyebrows flared into his forehead. "I need a few more *bottles* to mend." Picking an uncorked bottle of champagne from several on the table, he placed it to his lips then emptied the contents in a single draught. "Hey, Riz!" He slammed the green bottle onto the table. "You were right!"

Across the table, Risaliti wiped his chin with a sleeve. A cigarette thick with ash dangled from the corner of his mouth. "About?"

"You told us we're going to party like there's no tomorrow..." Moore grabbed a new bottle from a passing waitress. "And here we are!" Champagne bubbled over the edge of the bottle and the soldier thrust it to his lips.

Risaliti's weight shifted beneath a sizable French woman perched on his lap. She was built like a Sherman tank. Her curled, dark locks fell below thick shoulders and into the private's face. "That's great news, about Arthur. *Real* good news."

"Hey, Sarge," Piero shouted. "I heard the Germans blew up all b-b-but two bridges in town."

He squeezed Caro's hand. "Yeah, but we crossed the one that counted."

Moore pulled a fresh cigarette from his shirt pocket and tapped it against an open palm. "I hear the bulk of Germany's army has fled north toward Dijon. And we captured over two thousand soldiers. Don't ask me, but I think the master race is about to be mastered!"

"All I know is there are far less Nazis than before!" Piero said.

Moore struck a match on the table and muttered in a deadpan. "Fewer."

"*What?*" Piero asked.

"Fewer," Moore repeated.

"Whatever. But isn't it t-t-true, Sarge?" Piero rubbed his chin. "With highways b-b-blockaded and almost all bridges and railroads destroyed, we're stuck here a couple days?"

"It is," Frank answered. "Engineers are clearing the way, but that's the rumor."

"Four years..." Moore pinched the cigarette and pulled it from his lips. "That's how long it's been since Lyon's been liberated."

"Friends, I've an announcement." Risaliti swigged champagne and handed the bottle to the woman on his lap. "I'd like to introduce you all...all of you...to my future wife."

A corner of Piero's mouth ticked into a smile as he looked upon the woman's weathered face. "Nice to meet you, Mrs. Risaliti. The p-p-pleasure's ours." But she stared straight ahead, mesmerized by the crowded hall, oblivious to his words.

Haubert's arm draped over Moore's shoulder. Both privates eyed the woman's tanklike frame. "She's so purdy, she'd make a train take a dirt road." Haubert chuckled.

Moore's body threw back with laughter. His flying elbow butted an empty bottle, and it crashed to the floor. "That's a good one, Hobs!"

"We should be drinking S-s-scotch." Piero leaned back in his chair, almost tipping it over. "You never get a hangover from Scotch, unless you get stupid d-d-drunk."

"Maybe, we should toast the beautiful newlyweds?" Haubert jumped to his feet, almost losing his balance and toppling over the chair in front of him. He raised a champagne bottle high above his curly hair, and the other soldiers joined in salute. Everyone at the table lifted their glasses. A half-chewed cigar bounced in his mouth with each syllable. "To the prince of all princes, my dubby Riz, and his new princess." Haubert's face twisted in confusion as he plucked a piece of frayed tobacco from his mouth. "*Waz* her name?"

"Her name?" Risaliti cleared his throat. "Her name's..." His face sagged into a blank expression. Turning to the woman, he parted a wall of dark hair and whispered into her ear.

She ignored him and chugged the remaining contents before pounding the bottle onto the tabletop.

"Her name's not important... What's important is...who's hungry?" Risaliti heaved a sigh. His head slumped forward against her shoulder and his nose buried in her dark curls.

Moore clapped palms together, pressed hands onto the tabletop, and stood with unsteady legs. A cigarette, tucked in the corner of his mouth, dropped hanging ash into a champagne glass below. Apparently oblivious to the ash, he bolted down the contents then grabbed a full bottle, splashing a refill. "May I have your attention? I propose a *real* toast." Clearing his throat, Moore climbed on top of his chair and bellowed, "*A soldier's home is on the land. A sailor's home at sea. But a whiskey glass and a stripper's ass is home sweet home to me!*"

Soldiers roared with approval, even from nearby tables.

Frank glanced into Caro's eyes, ignoring the revelry surrounding him.

As the last pair of tumblers flipped from the stage, lights darkened. A lone spotlight shone in the middle of the stage. An emcee strolled into the spot holding a microphone. He uttered a few words of French, and a female singer wearing a black gown that swept the stage beneath her appeared out of the darkness. A red-flowered hair clip dangled from the side of her head.

Immediate hoots of approval reverberated from both the floor and balcony. She took the microphone and cradled it between both hands. A very feminine yet husky voice escaped her lips, and the musicians slowly joined. As she combined French with American lyrics, the audience fell spellbound. Noise and commotion dissipated, and the dance floor packed with soldiers and civilians.

Frank caressed a strand of Caro's hair with a single finger. "There's one thing I've been meaning to ask you. And not being able to is killing me."

Her large violet eyes widened.

"Would you dance with me?" Frank asked excitedly.

"*Oui.*"

The couple strode to the crowded dance floor and leaned into each other. Frank's right hand rested in Caro's left, his other pressed on her hip. Under hazy illumination, they swayed to the rhythm of the music until their movements became one.

"How's your mouth?" Frank asked.

Caro dabbed her bruised lip. "Sore but fine."

Pressing his to cheek to hers, he caught a scent of perfume. "When I lost you, I fell into some black, aching void. I didn't know if I'd ever find you, and I couldn't get over it."

Caro's head rested on his shoulder; her fingernails caressed the back of his neck.

"But you did find me," she said.

At last, he said, "I did."

"And now?" Caro said it in a voice so soft, Frank had to lean closer to hear.

"And now we're given one more night and I must leave...again."

"But nothing's changed, Frank. I'll be here, waiting for you."

"But the longer this war goes, the more I'm obsessed by one thought, getting back to you, and the longer it lasts, the less I believe I'll—"

"Don't. Don't *ever* talk like that," she snapped. "*You* need to believe it." Caro's hand cupped Frank's chin. She lifted and peered into his face. "You hear me, Sergeant Taylor? I'll be here when you return. *Believe it*, always."

He nodded. Then, his eyes opened wide as if he just remembered something important. "I've a gift for you." He reached into a shirt pocket and opened his hand. A few dried rose petals clustered in his palm. "Caro petals."

Her fingertip pressed against them. "*Caro* petals?"

"After you were taken, and before I left La Ciotat, I took one of the roses I cut for you from the vase. It's been in my pocket this entire time. These few petals are all that's left."

"But that's not true."

"What's not true?"

"You once told me, 'All will bloom again.' Don't you see, Frank? It's happening. Everything *is* blooming again. Soon, more flowers than you or I could count in a lifetime will blossom as our country returns to life. Our *world* returns to life."

Frank's lips met Caro's in the most delicate and tender of kisses. He pulled back and lost himself in her gaze. "I really thought I lost you. Yet, here I am holding you now. I'll never let you go again, Caro."

"Nor should you," she whispered.

His earlobe prickled from her warm breath. "From the first minute I saw you, I knew."

"Remember, Frank, inspiration sprung from love is the purest of things." On stage, the lyrics softened.

Frank bent to Caro's ear. "A thousand years..."

Her delicate eyebrows ticked up.

"I wish I could give you a thousand years."

"I'll take them," she said against his lips.

The song's final notes settled over the crowded hall, but the couple continued dancing as if only their world existed. Noise crescendoed into a dull roar, and soldiers shouted to be heard. A small chorus line of dancers climbed the stairs leading to the stage.

Frank took Caro's hand and led her back to the table, winding through the crowded dance floor. "Let's say goodbye to the boys and enjoy our night...*alone*."

When Frank returned to the table, his eyes jerked wide in disbelief. A familiar figure dressed in a frayed sweater, patched work pants, and battered field boots stood before him. "*Michael?*"

"Good to see you, little brother!"

"*Michael!* What the *hell* are you doing here?"

The brothers fell into a tight embrace. Frank lifted Michael off the floor and squeezed, before setting him down. "*Ohhh*, my back, be careful of my back." Michael grimaced in pain. "If I told you that story, Frank, I'd need a few days."

"Where's your uniform? Why're you dressed like that?"

"Again, very long story, for another time." Michael ran fingers playfully through Frank's curly hair. "But suffice it to say, the last few weeks have been the adventure of a lifetime."

"How'd you know I was here?"

"I didn't. I ran into one of your men who somehow thought I was you. I guess we brothers look alike, despite our dress."

Frank turned his head and smiled at Caro. "I've someone very special I'd like you to meet." She stepped to Frank's side. "This is Caro. She's the sister of a very dear friend, a French commando who served with our unit. His name's Arthur. He's recovering in the hospital, but he'll be fine."

Caro extended a hand. "A pleasure."

"The pleasure is mine, *mademoiselle*."

A champagne bottle crashed to the floor on the opposite side of the table. Haubert and Piero argued in heated fashion. "Why the hell would ya want ta know that?"

"I don't know! But I'd rather be throwing baseballs than grenades!" Piero slammed an empty bottle onto the table.

"Don't ya know what curiosity did to tha coon?" Haubert screamed.

"Don't you mean *c-c-cat*?"

"Doesn't matta! It ends in the same damn thing!"

Frank tapped his brother's shoulder and grabbed Caro's hand. "Let's get outta here. It's starting to get ugly."

"Before we go, I've someone I'd like you to meet." Michael wound between chairs and people everywhere, to a table in the back corner of the hall. One of the men, dressed in dark slacks, a blue shirt, and a beret, stood and shuffled to Michael's side. "This is Maurice. He's a large reason I'm still alive."

"Your brother's too kind," the Frenchman said, taking a long drag on a cigarette. "It was my and my men's pleasure. Come, let me introduce you to them."

"Yes, of course. And thank you, Maurice," Frank smirked. "I hope he wasn't too much trouble." Frank cupped his mouth so Maurice could hear. "I know he can be a *real* pain sometimes."

Around the hall, shouting replaced conversation, and shrieking replaced quiet laughter. A line of dancers kicked away on stage as musicians joined in the celebration.

"I'll be right back," Frank whispered to Caro.

Frank and Michael followed Maurice around the table. Maurice stopped next to a small man with a solid build. A dark goatee made his chin look as pointed as the tip of an arrow. "This is Felix," Maurice yelled. Felix glanced up from his chair, sipping champagne from a narrow glass. Maurice continued around the table. "Over here is Pierre and Jaques. They have been with us from the beginning." Both men, dressed in tattered sweaters and dark slacks, smiled contagiously. Their youthful cheeks radiated ruby red and signaled too much alcohol.

Frank patted Jacques on the back. "Nice to meet you. *Merci*, for helping my brother."

Trombones and trumpets blared away on stage.

"And finally, standing over there..." Maurice extended his arm and pointed. "We have Laurent, he's the short one, and Malory."

A crop of blond hair protruded under a black beret of the taller man. He stepped forward into a bright cone of light and nodded.

Frank glared at this Frenchman's face with a suspicious look. Something smacked familiar. *His eyes! One's blue, and the other...*

*****

Caro's body went liquid, her tongue drowned in fear. Breath caught in her throat. Finally, words stumbled from lips, but nothing more than an inaudible whimper escaped. "*C'est eux!*" Without warning, a blood-curdling scream burst deep within her. "*C'est eux!*" It's *them*! My God, Frank, it's them!" But the roar of the crowd, and blare of the band in full swing, smothered her cries.

The shorter man pointed at Caro and nudged the taller, whose eyes widened in fear.

Frank spun towards her. Caro screamed and shook her finger at the villains. "*Frank!*"

"What's wrong?" Michael mouthed, but his voice was lost in the din.

Frank's eyes turned back to the two men as the taller reached into his coat.

"Those two! They're Nazis! The ones who kidnap—"

But music overpowered from the nearby stage and muffled any word Caro spoke. Someone behind roared in laughter.

Caro snapped, sobbing, and out of breath. She screamed at the top of her lungs. "*It's them!*"

*****

Frank's hand reflexively lowered for his sidearm, but there was no gun. Guns were not needed at this celebration.

For an instant, Frank felt as if time had almost stopped. Terror shredded his mind, transforming him into action, but everything slowed to a torturous crawl.

"What's wrong?" Michael yelled.

Malory whipped out a pistol.

Frank knew he couldn't get to the gun in time. He hopped around chairs and darted between people.

On stage, dancers kicked away, and musicians blared chords. Everything blurred in a haze of smoke and celebration.

Malory's hate was palpable. He took aim at Caro. Fear leapt into his dark eyes as he fingered the trigger.

In a split second, Frank was out of time. Without hesitation, he hurled his body, arms thrown about Caro's neck. She stumbled backward but reached out and caught him. Their eyes locked together, just as moments earlier on the dance floor.

Maurice smashed a bottle over Malory's head, and he crumpled. Felix tackled Laurent. Other soldiers dove onto the piles. Fists pounded in fury.

Dancers on stage stilled, musicians gasped, and, throughout the hall, a hush enveloped the celebration.

Frank's arm hung about Caro's neck, and he smiled. "Are you okay?"

"I…I think so…I…" But Frank's hand slid from her cheek and dangled by his side.

Caro's legs sagged under the suddenness of his body weight.

A sickening warmth covered Frank's side. She opened a bloodied palm. "Mon Dieu! *Frank?*" Her eyes widened in terror.

A single word escaped his throaty gurgle. "Caro?" He tried to steady himself but slumped toward the floor.

"*Au secours, à l'aide!* We need *help*!" Tears streaked her eyes. "*Un médecin! Vite!*" Caro fell to her knees, still supporting the back of Frank's head. She lowered it into her lap and stared in horror.

Michael dropped to the floor beside his brother, his face mortified. He clutched his brother's hand. "Hang on, Frank. *Hang on*!" Taylor's men huddled around him.

"Sarge!" someone yelled.

"We *need* a doctor!"

"Someone, get a doctor!"

"Get help!"

Risaliti ripped off his jacket and pressed it against the spreading crimson on Frank's side.

Frank found her eyes and for a moment, everything was right. *I wish I could give you…* He raised a single finger to Caro's face and traced the outline of her nose and lips. "I would've forgiven you as well."

"*Forgiven* me?" Confusion and fear poured from Caro's face. "Forgiven me for *what*?"

Frank gasped, breathy and cold. "For stealing cookies." His finger fell to her chin, stilled, and collapsed onto his chest.

"*Frank!*" Her face hovered a breath away. The warmth of her touch comforted him. "Don't you leave me! You're going to be okay!" Caro's tears fell and washed across his cheek.

But when his eyes grew much too heavy, he closed them. *One thousand years.*

Her voice trailed into a whisper. "You *have* to believe! You *must*! Do you hear me? Stay with me! You have to—"

Caro's words blurred into a soft, electronic buzz. It heightened in pitch then diminished into numbing silence. Frank Taylor's life floated out of him like a silk handkerchief pulled from the warmth and safety of its own pocket, and one strange feeling dominated his being.

All is blue.

TWENTY-FIVE
Geneviève's Story

Five Years Later

An old woman stepped from the entrance of her farmhouse. A frayed coat hung on her frail form, and her oversized boots shuffled into lush grass. She carried a wooden bucket in each hand and strode to the middle of the yard. After setting one bucket down, she reached inside the other, grabbed a handful of feed, and scattered it to the ground. Grain fell between blades of thick green grass covering the area. In an instant, chickens, ducks, and turkeys flocked in every direction, blanketing the yard. The birds cackled and clucked in excitement as they fought for food.

"Easy, pretty ones. Plenty to go around."

Geneviève caught sight of a small chick pressed outside the circle of animals and pushed her way forward. "Some for you, too, little one." The old woman stooped low and dropped more feed as she continued to the barn, fifty yards behind the house. Geneviève entered and poured one of the buckets into a metal trough for two cows. They mooed their approval. A distinct odor of wooden rafter beams, stacks of hay bales, and animal pens blazed familiarly through her nostrils. In the rear of the barn, a horse popped its head out of the final stall. Geneviève stroked its muzzle and poured the remaining feed into a larger bucket. "Yes, Jeffrey, I've brought some for you, too."

A stack of dried firewood rested below leather horse harnesses hanging from a rusted nail driven into a wooden beam. Geneviève snatched a few pieces of wood, dropped them into the buckets, and strode to the farmhouse. She pushed the front door open with the toe of her boot and entered. At the kitchen table, an old man with a headful of white hair sat cross-legged, sipping from a beige cup and smoking an ivory pipe.

A broad grin crossed his face. "Another package arrived from our dear boy." An extended arm offered his wife a chair.

She lowered the buckets onto the floor, slipped off her boots, and eased into the seat next to him. "And what's our Michael sent this time?"

Albert scratched his chin and reached into a box perched in the middle of the table. The farmer pulled out a burlap sack and set it on the tabletop. "Our dear boy has sent..." His wrinkled hands disappeared into the sack and reemerged. "Three containers of coffee. Very strong, no doubt." He placed the containers to the side. "Two new pairs of work pants and two work shirts." Geneviève reached for the pants and shirts, pulling them into her arms. "And there's a leather purse." His fingers pulled out 750 francs.

The old woman stared at the money resting in the flat of her husband's palm then shook her head. "*C'est trop.*"

"Agreed. Too much." Albert smiled. "But he always sends too much." He folded the bills, tucked them into the hip pocket of his overalls, and nodded. "There's an envelope as well." His hands, weathered like used wax paper, ripped the envelope open and tugged at a letter. "*And* something inside." Tilting the paper, a silver chain with an attached medal slid into the farmer's palm. Albert handed the chain to his wife and read.

Dear Albert and Geneviève,

I trust this letter finds you well. It's hard to believe how quickly time passes. And as seasons change, there are many things that never will. Of those, my eternal thanks and gratitude for all you risked for me...a virtual stranger thrown into your lives by circumstance of war. I am doing well and find myself, as of now, the father of three beautiful sons, Daniel, Joel, and Rocco. I look forward to bringing them to France for our annual visit come fall.

Sarah is doing quite well, as is my mother, Maribeth, and father, Lawrence. They cherish the time spent with their grandchildren and love to spoil them as grandparents do. The amazing thing is that none of this would be possible if not for your unselfishness and bravery. I know you are probably thinking, "C'est trop." *But when you love someone, what you do for them, what you give them, or what you wish you could give them, can never be too much. Gifts from the heart are hardly ever enough.*

I have enclosed a medal of St. Peter, the rock of the church. In addition to honoring the memory of your son, it also honors the fact you both were my rock all those years ago. What you risked will never be forgotten by any generation of my family. Please take care, and we look forward to seeing you both soon.

Sincerely,

Michael

Albert folded the letter carefully, slipped it inside the envelope, and inhaled deeply on his pipe. Geneviève stood and walked to the wooden wall next to the cupboard. Candlelight danced on the silver links of the medal as it dangled from her arthritic fingers. She draped the chain over the crucifix hanging on the wall and looked over her shoulder. She caught Albert's eye and nodded. Inches from where the American once stood in fear, Geneviève placed a fingertip to the wall and traced seven splintered holes. But now, she and her husband fully understood their significance.

The constellation is called the Plough.

*****

Life in Thompsonville, Kansas, hadn't changed much in the last five years. Since taking over Uncle Luke's farm, Michael and Sarah prospered through hard work and fertile land. Taylor crops always delivered the best produce in town. While their family planted, gathered, and sold six days a week, Sundays were a time for family. After early morning Mass, Michael gathered his family for a picnic on the shores of Perry Lake.

The proud parents of three sons loaded a horse-drawn wagon with food, drink, and family, and headed for the lush fields. As the wagon weaved through the countryside, asters bloomed fully and lined the hills with starry-shaped purple heads. Verdant meadows and fields never seemed more alive. And when the blue lake came into sight, it never seemed clearer. Throughout the day, the family picnicked and played games. Michael taught his oldest, Daniel, how to fish and read the signs of nature. Sarah played with their two younger sons on the blanket shaded by a century oak tree. Little Joel learned how to walk over that blanket. A few weeks later, he ran. Baby Rocco watched precociously from his basket.

And when the sun set behind the lake and cast its golden light on all of God's creation, Michael loaded the wagon for home. Soon, over a million stars winked in the heavens. Bullfrogs lined muddy edges of riverbanks, croaking their approval. The family breathed in the light airy scent of the wilderness and a day well spent. As the horse trudged forward, tugging at the wagon, constellations crowned their heads.

"Father?" Daniel gazed at the night sky. "Where do stars come from?"

"Well, some people say stars are rays of light that travel millions of miles to earth." Michael held the reins with one hand and squeezed Sarah's hand with the other. "But I like to think they're a reminder. A reminder of something grand, of something much bigger than us. And if you can read their signs, they'll always lead you in the right direction."

Sarah kissed her husband's cheek and leaned into his shoulder.

"It kind of makes you think, Daniel, that if God had time to make something as wonderful as the stars in the heavens, we must be pretty important, too."

*****

A framed black-and-white photograph of two young, grinning boys, climbing a haystack, rested on the nightstand next to her. An envelope leaned against the frame. Maribeth climbed into bed and caught sight of the photo. She smiled to herself, for the image of her sons was as clear in her mind as any she could ever remember. Rolling over in bed, she draped an arm around her sleeping husband. "Good night, Lawrence," she whispered.

And she never slept more sound.

TWENTY-SIX

Lambrecht's Story

Hanz paused between house and workshop. Glancing to his right, then left, the sheer scale of mountain slope to valley hinted paradox. An abundance of verdancy shrouded the countryside. Varied flora and fauna lined a lush green carpet throughout the valley of the Rhine. His initial thought leaned toward a hint of sublime and feeling of awe.

To live in Liechtenstein means residing in nature herself.

His lungs filled with fresh mountain air as he pushed open the door to his father's workshop. Easing into the chair, he reached for a newspaper on the workbench. The yellowed paper was dated June 24, 1945. Glancing at the headline, he read out loud. "Colonel Friedrich Richter guilty. Execution set." Hanz flipped the paper to another page and scrolled to the bottom. In small print, a faint sentence caught his eye. "Captain William Lambrecht killed in Berlin bombing." Hanz closed the paper and dropped it onto the workbench.

He strode to the corner of the shop and grabbed a stepladder. Placing it under one of the rafters, he climbed. On a shelf above his head, a small wooden box rested next to a gray one. Hanz slid the gray one into his hands and climbed down. He pulled the lid off to uncover a layer of white tissue paper. As he pushed the paper aside, a pair of knee-high, form-fitted ebony boots revealed themselves. Hanz smiled to himself as he stared at the immaculate boots.

Danke, Father.

He reached for the newspaper, dropped it onto the boots, and covered everything with white tissue paper. He closed the lid, climbed the ladder, and slid the gray box next to the wooden one. Hanz returned the ladder to the corner of the room and shut the light off, exiting the workshop. Outside, the sun radiated on his face and arms. Despite the warm month, snow capped the mountains six thousand feet above and ringed the valley below in a massive precipice of stone.

This is the natural grandeur of God's country.

Hanz pushed the door open and walked into the house. "*Mother?*" An aroma of pastry and pie wafted in the air. "Anna? Frances?"

A voice rang from the kitchen. "We're in here...baking".

"Where's little William?" Hanz asked.

"In his room taking a nap." Hanz walked to his eleven-year-old's room and cracked the door open. The small boy slept soundly, curled around a teddy bear. Hanz smiled to himself and strolled downstairs to the kitchen. Mother pulled a tray of freshly baked apple pies from the oven. She tugged a single cooking mitt off and dipped one arthritic finger into the side of a pie.

"Using your magic pinky, Mother?" Hanz asked.

"You know my thermometer."

"I know your cooking's truly a slice of heaven."

She pushed the tray back into the oven. "*Danke,* my son. Remember, even in the smallest of tasks, always strive for perfection." Eva wiped a hand onto an already-stained cooking apron. "Would you like a piece of warm apple pie, my son?"

Frances snatched a plate and fork from a cupboard as Hanz settled into a chair at the table. "Pies are for angels, dear Father."

A sly smile crossed his face. "*So,* I'm an angel?"

Anna chuckled. "Today." She cut a piece of pie, plated it, and placed it in front of her husband. "*Tomorrow?*"

Eva leaned in and kissed her son's cheek. "You'll always be my angel." She spun around and continued peeling apples.

Hanz stared at the back of his mother's, wife's, and daughter's forms as if taking a mental snapshot. The women stood there working, silhouetted by oven and trays of pastry. Hanz pressed the image into his mind. Frances hummed a song from childhood, and the heat emanating from the oven radiated against their bodies.

Hanz grabbed a fork and cut into the apple pie. He placed it to his lips and tasted the sweetness. *Delicious...simply delicious. "Kutchen himmel!"* he proclaimed.

The three women looked back over their shoulders and smiled. Love, family, and contentment found its way into the smallest corner of civilization.

Pie Heaven, indeed, Hanz concluded.

And the power of Liechtenstein's nature fulfilled its promise, healing any wound, visible or not.

TWENTY-SEVEN
Arthur's Story

Leaning forward against the thrust of oars in the water, he rowed into the harbor. With the sun directly overhead, the best fishing hours were gone. Its direct rays beat onto the back of his neck and arms with a pulsing sensation. Though his lower back ached dully from sitting on a wooden thwart, it had been a productive morning.

Four good fish will make excellent meals.

Arthur peered into the water. Its clarity and blueness always soothed his spirit.

"You were very kind today," Arthur said out loud. He frequently talked to the ocean. Its familiarity was one of a friend in whom he confided. His father had done the same. Charles coaxed the sea on fishless days and blessed her on successful ones. "And so, I thank you." He recalled the first time Father had brought him fishing. "I was six," he muttered. "And I was so excited I could not sleep. Father taught me how to tie a proper knot, and I swelled with pride. He treated me like a man from that day forward."

Oars dipped and pushed as the tiny rowboat slipped through the harbor's entrance. Anchored boats already lined the docks. Each hull a different color, creating a rainbow just above the water's surface. Arthur gazed to his left. Perched on the absolute edge of the coastline, a monolith of gray stone thrust itself five-hundred feet skyward. The sheer size of it was comparable to that of a small island.

Father's favorite fishing spot was tucked inside its protective shadow.

The menacing facade of stone affirmed what Arthur had always believed. La Ciotat was truly a marriage of land and sea, a loving consequence of Earth's embrace.

Petite Fleur slid between two other rowboats, and Arthur moored her to the dock. He unclipped the stringer from the frame and stepped off the boat. *I'll return later for the equipment.* He strode across the dock and leapt ashore, a slight limp in his gait.

An old man sat cross-legged at a crowded outdoor café, reading a newspaper. He sipped from a small cup and yelled in Arthur's direction. "Nice catch!"

Arthur smiled. "*Merci.*" He tilted his head, eyed the heavens, and breathed. Fresh air filled his lungs as he admired three dominant colors directly in front of him. Beige buildings, green hills, and blue sky. Below, his feet clicked on the cobblestone road that wound up the hill and into the heart of town. Arthur passed a general store and floral shop, both bustling with activity.

Across the street, a woman built like a broomstick scurried behind a fruit-and-vegetable stand. Apples, oranges, bananas, pears, and grapes striped the cart with a spectrum of colors as a line of customers waited their turn. Arthur swung the stringer to his other shoulder and, for no particular reason, recalled a childhood tune. It was a comforting song *Mère* once sang to him and Caro during thunderstorms.

An aroma of fresh-baked bread wafted in the air before he even walked through the entrance. Aunt Margaret, built like a loaf of boule, stood behind a counter of freshly baked croissants and bagels. Reaching over the counter, she handed a brown bag overflowing with fresh bread to a young woman. "*Arthur!*"

The woman turned to leave and noticed the stringer on Arthur's shoulder. "Nice fish."

"*Merci,*" Arthur chuckled. "It was as if they jumped on my line today."

The woman smiled and walked out the door.

Arthur threw his arms open, the fish dangling from his outstretched hand. “And how is my aunt doing today?”

“*Mon cher!*” With a smudge of flour on her chin, Margaret waddled around the counter. An immaculate apron covered her wide form. She embraced her nephew with a tight squeeze and planted two quick kisses on his cheek. “I see fishing went well today?”

“Quite. Would you like one?”

“Ohhh, *merci*!” Margaret’s shrill voice echoed in the store. “Just put it in the icebox for now.”

Arthur strode to the back of the shop and placed the stringer inside the refrigerator.

“Fresh bread’s almost ready.” Margaret pulled a chair up and eased into it. “But first, I rest.”

Arthur stared with concern as he sat next to her. “Are you well, my dear aunt?”

“*Ça va*. Business is excellent...but I miss him. Every day.”

“As we all do.” Arthur rubbed the old wound in the leg he had once broken.

Margaret’s hands folded together over Arthur’s. “More importantly, how’ve *you* been, my dear nephew?”

“I can’t lie. Life was quite difficult at first. Losing so many you love.” Arthur leaned back in his chair and stared at the shimmering heat escaping the oven. “War is like some swift river, and once you’re caught in its current, you can’t escape. It carries you downstream, and no matter how hard you fight, escape is impossible. When you finally do emerge, if you’re lucky enough, it’s like you’re still...not clean. And definitely not the boy you were when it started.” He broke his gaze from the oven and squeezed his aunt’s hands. “But being home, with passage of time, and having my own family now, I’m beginning to feel whole, and most content." The two sat in silence for a moment until a large smile crossed Arthur's face and he chuckled.

"*What?* What's so funny, Nephew?"

"I remember when Caro and I would stop after school. Uncle Jean would treat us to anything we wanted."

"He liked to spoil you."

"And, I *still* remember his five commandments for bakers." Arthur reached across the table and wiped a smudge of flour from his aunt's cheek.

"Ohhh, that's right," Margaret squealed.

"*Premier commandement.* Give a man a roll, feed him a day, but teach a man to bake?" Arthur patted his stomach. "Feed him a lifetime."

Margaret nodded, smiling.

"*Deuxième commandement.* Not all bread"—Arthur raised his index finger for emphasis—"is created equal."

"*Le troisième?*"

"One cannot rush a good bread."

"*Et le quatrième?*"

"Warm bread warms the heart!"

The fleshy roll of skin under Margaret's neck jiggled as she chuckled. "And *et le cinquième?*"

Arthur paused then declared triumphantly, "Everything is good in moderation!"

"That's right. Do not sample everything!" A hearty laugh blurted from the woman's lips, and she patted her own stomach. "Or you look like me, a loaf of boule. Are you headed home now?"

"*Oui.* Cate waits patiently for me to bring dinner."

"And how is the little one?"

"Little Adam is like most four-year-olds...curious."

Margaret placed both hands flat on the tabletop and pushed herself to her feet. "And that is the way you want boys, *curious.*" She walked to the oven, pulled the handle down, and peeked inside. "Almost ready."

Arthur walked to the refrigerator, unhooked a fish, and pulled the stringer out. He returned to his aunt, leaned down, and kissed her on the cheek. "I'll see you tomorrow."

"Very well. Don't forget to take a loaf for dinner."

"Of course." Arthur grabbed a warm loaf of baguette with his left hand while carrying the stringer in his right and strolled toward the door. "*Au revoir*, Aunt Margaret."

He glanced to the right. A solitary, immaculate apron hung from a wooden peg. He thought of Uncle Jean and his commandments. Pushing the door open, he walked onto the street and turned for home. Pale sandstone buildings with black ironwork balconies lined the cobblestone road. Stepping into sunlight, he absorbed the radiating warmth. Michael pursed his lips together and whistled the melody etched in his heart.

It was the song that *Maman* had sung to her children when they were frightened by an oncoming storm.

A rising joy crept into his heart. And for the first time in many years, Arthur Lambert exhaled, cleansed of all anxiety.

TWENTY-EIGHT
Lucy's Story

The five-year-old's small strides clicked rhythmically down the path. A silver locket bounced around her neck, shimmering in the sunlight. Her short raven hair bobbed against shoulders as she breathed in the sweet summer air with a happy hum.

At the water's edge, Lucy raised a hand to shield her eyes from the setting sun's glare made especially sharp by the water's reflection. Dancing around the corner of the weathered boathouse, she aimed for the wooden door and shoved it open with both hands. She skipped toward the ladder and grasped a bottom rung.

Lucy giggled and counted the last rungs she climbed as if playing a game. "*Trois...deux...un!*" At the top of the ladder, she flung herself into the loft.

The bed of straw tickled her bare knees as she crawled. A figure appeared in the far corner of the loft, staring through a small hole in the ceiling above her head. A single tile of terracotta roof leaned against the wall. "I knew you'd be here!"

"You did?"

Lying next to her mother, Lucy wiggled close. "What're you staring at?"

Mother's arm wrapped around her. "I'm waiting for the first star."

"Uncle says stars are made of fire." Lucy giggled. "Like candles that burn at church."

"What do *you* say stars are made of?" Her mother turned on her side, leaned on an elbow, and smiled.

Lucy's eyes blinked in amazement at the twilight sky. A slanted ray of light bathed her face. "I think...I think they are eyes of angels. And every night they sparkle in happiness." Her words were filled with all the wonder of Christmas morning.

"A big thought for such a little girl." A strand of dark hair fell into Lucy's face, and Mother brushed it away with a tender touch.

"Merci, Maman."

Lucy and her mother lay in silence holding hands when a voice boomed just outside the boathouse.

"Where's my daughter? *Where's* my Lucy?"

The little girl giggled and buried her head into her mother's bosom. Lucy heard a figure climb the ladder top and jump into the loft.

"Lucille, you *forgot* something."

Lucy turned wide-eyed. "What, *Papa*? What did I forget?"

"You forgot this." Her father placed a cardboard box into tiny outstretched hands.

The child squealed in delight. "*La cigale!*" She set the box onto the straw bedding and peered inside. "The one we caught this afternoon. But I want to hear him sing!"

"That's right," Mother said. "Then we must always release them. Remember, they'll never sing in captivity. They want to be free, like us." Mother's hand extended for Father's, and their fingers intertwined.

Lucy glanced at her father.

"Go ahead, honey." Father nodded approval. "Pick it up."

She reached inside the box, brushed aside a sunflower, and enveloped the cicada. Lucy moved under the aperture in the ceiling and extended her right arm. As she opened her hand, the cicada perched for a moment as if trained to do so. Suddenly, the insect's wings fluttered to life, and it flew through the opening, and disappeared into the twilight. "*Liberté!*" A smile beamed on Lucy's face. "It flies, *Maman*!" She giggled. "It flies, *Papa*!"

Father leaned into Mother's shoulder. He brushed a strand of dark hair behind her ear.

"It *flies*!" Lucy stood and peered through the roof. "It flies to the setting sun!" She pulled her head back and sank into the straw. "*Maman*, sing for me. *Please!*"

Mother's violet eyes found Father's and then Lucy's.

"*Please!*" Lucy squealed again.

"Very well. But first..." Mother patted the straw. "Lie down, next to us." Three forms lay in the loft of the boathouse. Their bodies pressed against each other, searching the cloudless twilight sky from the flat of their backs. Lucy's chest thumped with anticipation.

"I will sing for my lovely daughter, Lucille. And I will sing for my most handsome husband, Frank." Her mother breathed in, and, when silence gave way to voice, the sound seemed incredibly large and filled the loft with an angelic presence.

Au clair de la lune
Mon ami Pierrot
Prête-moi ta plume
Pour écrire un mot

Mother's words washed over Lucy and through her being. And in the loft, at that moment, she prayed to God to always be this happy.

Ma chandelle est morte,
Je n'ai plus de feu
Ouvre-moi ta porte
Pour l'amour de Dieu.

Father sat up, leaned on one elbow, and stared at Lucy and Mother. A smile engulfed his face. "I have known, Caro..." he breathed. "I have *always* known."

*****

Through the aperture, across the bay, and over boats of many colors, Caro's song lingered after the *cigale*, flying through fragrant air. Her words echoed against the great hunchback of rock and scaled the jagged summit of Le Bec D'Aigle. From mountain to sky, her song slipped into the heavens and past the silver-lined stars that illume the earth. And no shadow, no matter how large, could ever fall upon her words, or her world, again.

As the setting sun splashed final light onto terracotta roofs, sides of buildings illuminated, boats, and waters shimmered, and children's faces glowed. In this small corner of the universe, all was right in La Ciotat.

For Frank Taylor, the war was over.

Made in the USA
Columbia, SC
03 October 2021